The Amateur

Robert Ledford

Copyright © 2010 Robert Ledford

ISBN 978-1-60910-262-3

All rights reserved. No part of this book may be used or reproduced in any manner whatsoever without written permission, except in the case of brief quotations embodied in critical articles and reviews.

Printed in the United States of America.

The characters and events in this book are fictitious. Any similarity to real persons, living or dead, is coincidental and not intended by the author.

BookLocker.com, Inc.
2010

Cover design by Dave Averdick

Dedicated to a certain girl and her family. I'm sorry.

Chapter 1

It was the day before Valentine's Day, Friday the thirteenth. There were two boxes in my left coat pocket, similar in size, the primary difference being that the engagement ring in one cost significantly more than the Tic Tacs in the other. The whole day at work I'd worn my thick coat, refusing to take it off, and more than one person said I looked like an idiot. It may have been paranoia, but I wasn't comfortable leaving something that was worth more than my car in the glove compartment. Hanging up my coat wasn't an appealing option, either, considering the times I'd gone out for drinks with the guys in the office, most of whom would rather put their wife on the street than pick up a check.

A cynic might say I was cheap; giving my future wife a combination engagement ring and Valentine's Day gift, but it was part of my cloak-and-dagger act. I'd bought the ring at the beginning of the year, but the way I saw it, booking a hotel in the middle of January less than ten miles from our apartment was about as obvious as asking her to accompany me to the jewelry store. A romantic holiday weekend wouldn't so much as raise a blip on her radar.

My girlfriend, MaryAnn, is a head turner; five-feet three with long, kinky-blonde hair, clear blue eyes, and a hypnotic way of moving her hips that could rock a man to sleep. We had met three years earlier when I was twenty-six and working for a large finance company. From the day she was hired, all of the single guys competed for her like we were on "The Bachelorette: Office Edition." The gods must have figured I was due because I was the lucky winner.

The gods definitely owed me. My name is Houston Hornsby Thomas, and believe it when I say there's a lot of trauma involved with have a last name for a first name, and vice versa. Every job application I've filled out has been handed back with instructions to put my last name first. Almost every credit card I've received has listed my name as Thomas Houston. On more than one occasion, I've asked my father why he couldn't just give me a regular white-bread American name, but he doesn't understand the problem. He was stationed in Houston, Texas when I was born and my name was meant to serve as a reminder of those great times. My middle name of Hornsby is the same as his. My grandfather was a big St. Louis Cardinals fan, and his favorite player was Rogers Hornsby. My dad says I should be thrilled to be named after a Hall-of-Famer. I'd have been happier if he'd named me after Jack the Ripper, or John the Baptist, or even Hugh the mailman.

MaryAnn and I dated for close to a year before getting a place together, and since then I'd played around with the idea of proposing. After some careful deliberation, I took a loan from my 401k account, and picked out a ring. Our first date had been on Fountain Square in downtown Cincinnati, Ohio, and it was there that I planned to pop the question.

I got home from work a little after five, and MaryAnn was waiting by the door, all of our stuff in an industrial-size gym bag.

"Cab will be here in a few minutes," she said, standing on tiptoe to give me a kiss. Almost on cue, a horn honked in the parking lot. I ran to the bedroom to change out of my work clothes, and was in the process of zipping up my jeans when the horn honked again.

"He said the meter's running," MaryAnn called out from the front door.

"Not doing his tip any favors," I muttered. I stepped into a pair of running shoes and headed out the door.

The cabbie was one of those older, thuggy-looking Italian guys with heavy jowls, shoe-black dyed hair and long sideburns, still in denial that the seventies were over. The once over he gave me screamed "why in the world is this girl with him?"

Admittedly, I'm no fashion model, but it's not like my head needs to be fitted for a paper bag, either. If I had to come up with a description for myself, I'd say I was on the good-looking side of average: about six-feet one, a hundred eighty-five pounds, brown hair, and the kind of blue eyes that one of my more enlightened ex-girlfriends had called "smoldering."

"Where to, boss?" he asked through the toothpick wedged in the right corner of his mouth. MaryAnn was in suspense as well.

"The Westin, downtown Cincinnati," I said.

"Very nice," MaryAnn murmured into my shoulder.

Downtown is a fifteen-minute ride from our apartment in Northern Kentucky, and we were in the middle of a conversation about where we would eat dinner when I said, "Sometimes I wonder if our lives are going in different directions."

MaryAnn's head which had been resting against my shoulder only a few seconds earlier was now facing straight forward, her neck rigid, and shoulders pulled back. My plan was to steer her toward believing I was breaking things off and then give her the good news; kind of taking her from one extreme to the other.

The cabbie dropped us off at our hotel, and after checking in and dropping off the gym bag, we took the short walk to the Starbucks on Fourth and Vine. Neither of us was talking, and it didn't take a brain surgeon to figure out that she was still ticked off by what I'd said earlier.

We got our customary mochas and started toward Fountain Square, which was a little over a block away. One of our traditions during the winter was to walk to the Square and sit at one of the tables, drinking our coffee in what was usually a vain attempt to stay warm.

I could feel a nervous anticipation as we made our way to the Fountain, and I tried to figure out how she would react once I'd proposed. I looked around, wanting to remember every detail. It was a cold day, even for February; probably in the low teens. The sun was nowhere to be seen, and the sky was overcast, gray in every direction. A lone ice-skater was making circles in the outdoor rink nearby, and a few bums shuffled by slowly, almost in place. The statue of the bronze woman on the Fountain had her arms opened wide, like she was waiting for an embrace.

I stopped and looked into her eyes. "There's something I've been thinking about lately, almost obsessively."

"Okay," she said, more as a question.

I reached into my coat pocket and grabbed hold of the box. "The thing is: I don't want you to be my girlfriend anymore."

I was about to say I wanted her to be my wife; the words were even forming on my lips, but before I could get them out she poked me hard in the chest.

"You smug bastard," she said. I tried to interrupt, but she poked me again. "For your information, I've been seeing a guy for the last three months and he's everything you're not. He's considerate, he's easy to talk to, and he's a hell of a lot better in bed."

I tried to think of something to say, but all I could do was open and close my mouth like a guy with lockjaw trying to chew gum. Seeing my shocked expression, she gave me a cold smile. "What are you obsessively thinking about now, you arrogant prick?"

I pulled the ring out of my pocket, looked at it, and then back at her. "I was trying to propose," I whispered, saying it more to myself.

I made my way over to the marble hedge surrounding the front part of the square and sat down. Even though I knew it was cold, I didn't feel it. I couldn't feel anything.

MaryAnn walked over and sat beside me. "I'm sorry," she said softly, her eyes on the ground.

I raised my eyebrows. "I was about to say I didn't want you to be my girlfriend anymore because I wanted you to be my wife."

We sat there for a long moment, neither of us saying anything. She finally looked up. "I was just trying to hurt you like you were hurting me," she said.

I put the ring back into my pocket and got to my feet. "I should probably take you home."

"What are you going to do?" she asked, eyes moist.

"I'll get my stuff together and move into a hotel while we sort it all out," I said, mustering what little dignity I had left.

MaryAnn kept glancing over while the cabbie drove us home, looking like she wanted to say something, but staying quiet. Tons of questions were running through my mind, but I didn't say anything, either. We pulled into the parking lot, and after tipping the cabbie a five, I sat on the front steps leading into our building.

"Are you coming in?" she asked.

She stood there, waiting for a response, but after a few seconds of silence she started toward the apartment. I turned to watch her walk up the stairs, thinking back to before I'd first asked her out. One of the things I'd always loved was watching her walk away. She had such an attitude about it, almost defiance.

After slapping the step where I was sitting until I could barely feel my hands, I walked into the apartment. MaryAnn was sitting on the couch next to the front door, and I walked past like she wasn't there. I retrieved my shaving kit from the bathroom and added in a toothbrush and a tube of toothpaste. Next, I went into our bedroom and grabbed a few pairs of underwear, a sweatshirt, some socks, and a couple pairs of jeans and threw it all into a Kohl's shopping bag that had been sitting against the wall. I was walking toward the door when it struck me that the situation with the guy was something she made up.

I looked out the window, feeling like an idiot. The whole cheating thing had to be untrue. If she'd really been messing around it would have been obvious.

The bedroom door opened. "It was a mistake," MaryAnn said, almost pleading. "I swear I was going to break it off anyway."

No way could I believe it was something she made up now. "Do what you want," I said, pushing by.

She put out a hand to stop me, but I pretended not to notice. I drew a small measure of satisfaction knowing it was my decision to leave; a very small measure, though, since she'd done the cheating.

I put the bag into the passenger seat of my car and after briefly considering going back to the hotel I'd booked for what was supposed to be our romantic weekend, I decided to just drive to the Motel 6 a few miles down the road. I got a room and just as I was placing my bag on the queen-sized bed, a semi drove by sounding like it was about to come through the wall. I thought about going down to the office and getting a room on the opposite side of the motel, but I knew there wasn't much point since I wouldn't sleep anyway.

I lay down on the bed for a few minutes, stared at the ceiling long enough to know I didn't want to stare at the ceiling all night, and then went searching for the nearest bar. A pool hall was only a stone's throw from the motel. The place was almost empty except for a few young guys shooting pool. I made a slow walk to the end of the bar furthest from the entrance. The bar stools had probably been there since the place first opened, and the vinyl covering them was sticking up in several places. I took a seat on the stool that looked to be in the best condition and the bartender made his way over. He could have been anywhere between forty and sixty, and the expression on his face said he'd seen it all.

"Johnnie Walker Red, straight up," I said.

As I watched him pour the shot, the reality of the situation started to sink in. The girl I thought would love me forever was probably this minute knocking boots with some other guy. The worst part was that all the signs were there. During the last six months, she'd started taking yoga twice a week, and was working in her classroom until six or seven o'clock every night. No mystery now on why she was gone so much.

I quickly swallowed the shot before he could walk away, and pointed at the empty shot glass.

"Make the next one a double," I said.

"You alright, buddy?" he asked as he placed the glass in front of me and filled it with whiskey.

"Women," I said, giving him a shrug.

"Half the reason I have a job," he said.

It took two swallows to toss down the double, and eyes watering, I pointed at the empty glass. Right about the time he poured my next drink, a middle-aged woman entered the pool hall. After surveying the bar area for several moments, she walked over and sat down, one stool between us. The alcohol was starting to work its magic, and I smiled at her through the mirror over the bar.

"How you doing?" I asked after she'd ordered an extra dry martini. The bartender shot me an amused glance as he mixed her drink.

She checked me out from head to toe. "Oh, I'm doing just fine," she said, putting something a little extra in her voice. "How are you?"

She wasn't too bad looking; a little chunky and maybe too much makeup, but not all that bad.

"I've been better," I said.

"You want to talk about it?" she asked.

I leaned toward the bar and turned the glass in my hands a few times. "I just broke up with my girlfriend."

"You poor thing," she said, a little too sympathetic. "Do you want another drink?"

I looked at her for a few seconds and then moved to the stool which had previously separated us.

"Only if you let me buy you one, too," I said.

One thing led to another and less than an hour later we were weaving our way back to my motel. We walked into the room and before I could take off my coat she was shedding clothes. By the time I slipped off my shoes and sweatshirt, she was completely naked and on all fours on the bed. Right about then, I had a moral dilemma. It didn't take a genius to figure out that this woman had been through more than a couple one-night stands, and I didn't have any sort of protection. Standing there, I couldn't even think of her name.

She turned and looked at me expectantly. "Is everything okay?"

I tried to look sheepish. "Uh, this isn't something I planned on, and I didn't bring any, you know…"

"Oh, no problem," she said. She grabbed her purse off the nightstand, rummaged through it for a few seconds and produced two condoms of what was obviously at least a three pack; casual about it, like she was handing me a pack of gum.

After it was over she lay next to me, her head on my shoulder. "Do you feel better?" she asked, stroking my chest.

I'm sure she expected the traditional, "oh yeah, baby" line, but she asked during the ten-minute period after sex where it doesn't even cross my mind to lie. "Not much would help at this point," I said. "We were together for three years."

"I like a man who is honest with me," she said. Her tone suggested that was clearly not the case.

I stared contemplatively at the ceiling. "I think this basically reaffirms what I've always said. I'm cursed."

"It can't be that bad," she said, her hand drifting slowly down my stomach.

"You'd be surprised," I said. I thought about pushing her hand away, but instead shifted slightly so that her hand was on my hip. "My life has been a long, non-stop disaster."

She laughed. "How's that?"

"Imagine two locomotives colliding at full speed." I brought my hands together to give the full effect. "The moment of impact, that's a snapshot of my life."

"No one's life is that bad."

"To start with, there's my name. Did I tell you my name before?"

She stopped touching me and looked up. Needless to say, the moment was a little awkward. "My first name is Houston, just like the city."

"As in, 'Houston, we have a problem,'" she said, like she was speaking into a microphone.

I tried to smile. "Yeah, just like that."

"I'm Valerie," she said, saying it like we were being introduced at a convention. I almost stuck out my hand.

"My life hasn't been great, either," she sighed. "First, I have three kids with a man who never pays child support, and he only sees them when that slut he married decides it's convenient. Then he acts like..."

"I'm sorry," I interrupted, "you said three kids?"

"Yeah, two boys a girl," she said brightly, reaching for her purse. "Here, I have some pictures."

I was thinking about all of the places I'd rather be at that moment. "No, that's all right," I said.

"That's not a problem, is it?"

"Why would it be a problem?" I asked. Obviously, the ten minutes were up.

"Most of the guys I date don't like the fact that I have children. Some men are such assholes."

"I guess so," I said. I made a point of yawning. "I'm sorry to do this to you, but I need to get some sleep."

There was an indignant expression on her face. "Are you asking me to leave?"

"Of course not," I said. "That would make this some kind of cheap one-nighter, and God knows we don't want that."

"Okay," she said, obviously missing the sarcasm. She got up and started toward the bathroom.

"If you need to get home to your kids, I completely understand," I called after her. She didn't answer until she got back.

"The kids are at their father's for the weekend," she said, climbing in next to me. "In fact, I have the whole weekend free, an empty house and no one to share it with." Obviously an invitation.

I tried to look disappointed. "I wish that person could be me, but I have to be in Cleveland in the morning. That's where my folks live, and we always spend Valentine's Day together."

I almost cringed after the words came out of my mouth. It was a horrible lie, but the only one I could come up with on the spot.

"Maybe when you get back then?"

"Definitely," I said, getting up and heading toward the bathroom. I shut the door behind me and stared at the mirror.

"You, my friend, are an idiot," I said to my reflection. I tried to think of a way to get out of climbing back into bed with that woman; Valerie, or whatever she said her name was, but the only alternative I could come up with was hanging myself from the shower curtain rod.

After a second glance at the shower curtain rod, I washed myself thoroughly with soap and water. Even though I'd worn a condom, it never hurt to be safe. I then relieved myself and reluctantly returned to bed. She attempted small talk, but when I didn't respond she eventually fell asleep. I listened to her measured breathing and stared up at the ceiling.

I was a twenty-nine year old male with no real prospects. My job was miserable, my love life was in shambles, and I was lying next to a woman old enough to be my mother.

I nodded off to sleep and a little while later woke up when the bed started creaking. My one-night stand was trying to get up quietly, but was making enough noise to wake the dead.

"Oh, hi," she said, acting perky. "I was going to get a shower and head out."

I propped myself up with an elbow. "Sure, go ahead."

I put my head back down on the pillow when she went into the bathroom, but the sound of the pipes in the shower coupled with the eighteen-wheelers driving by made it impossible to get back to sleep. The clock showed it was a little before eight, and I groaned as I searched through the sheets for my boxers. They were lying on the floor at the foot of the bed.

About ten minutes later she came out of the bathroom naked as the day she was born. Now that I was sober, I changed my mind about her wearing too much makeup. Without it, she looked like she was closing in on fifty.

I got in the shower, hoping that she'd be gone by the time I got out. It was about fifteen minutes later when I opened the door a crack to see if she was gone, but she was sitting on the bed, her feet dangling off the side. I started to close the door, but she made eye contact and waved so I wrapped a towel around my waist and gave her an embarrassed smile.

"I didn't want to leave without saying goodbye," she said, walking over and putting both of her arms around my waist.

"Oh, okay," I said, turning away. "If you want I'll drive you back to your car."

There was a disappointed frown on her face, but she shook her head. "It's not far."

There were a few awkward moments as we traded looks back and forth. "Here, let me give you my number," she said, reaching for her purse.

"Why don't you just tell it to me?"

Her eyebrows wrinkled. "You sure you don't want me to write it down?"

"I have a really good memory."

She gave me a number which I forgot by the time that she got the last digit out of her mouth. I crossed over to open the door and then gave her the same kiss on the cheek that I usually reserved for my grandmother.

"Thanks for a great night," I said, trying to sound sincere.

"I'll never forget it."

"Yeah, me either," I said. She stood there for a few more awkward moments and then walked out.

"Me, either," I muttered again after I closed the door.

Chapter 2

After my one-night stand was gone, I gathered my stuff together and headed back to the apartment. Maybe in time I could learn to forget what MaryAnn had done. Besides, anyone could make a mistake. Even before the previous night I knew that.

The weather was miserable when I left the motel. A wet, rainy snow was falling, and a mixture of slush and water covered the ground. I slogged my way to the car, trying to keep my shopping bag from getting in the muck. Traffic was at a crawl my entire drive home.

There was a brief moment of apprehension when I got to the door, and I wondered if I was about to walk in on something I didn't want to see. I started to stick my key in the lock, thought better of it, and rapped on the door. MaryAnn opened it a minute or so later, and believe it when I say a minute is a lot longer than it sounds.

As I walked in, the first thing I noticed was a pillow and sleeping bag lying on the couch. Her eyes darted toward the bathroom at the precise moment that a tall, skinny man emerged wearing only a towel. Upon seeing me, he didn't change expression; just reopened the bathroom door and disappeared inside.

"I was trying to catch you before you left this morning, but it appears I caught you in the act instead," I said cleverly. I turned to leave, but she grabbed my arm.

"Do you want to know why he's here?" she asked. I looked at her without responding, but didn't pull away. "I asked him to come over so I could end it, but by the time we finished talking he said he was too tired to drive home. I swear nothing happened. He even slept on the couch." She pointed toward the sleeping bag as proof.

"You swear you broke it off?" I asked.

"Swear to God."

I pretended to study her, but I wanted to believe her so I did. "I guess there are some things we need to talk out," I said, looking at the bathroom.

"He's leaving as soon as he gets dressed."

I looked down at my left wrist even though I wasn't wearing a watch. "Be back in an hour."

"I'm sorry," she said softly.

"Yeah," I muttered.

There was a McDonalds not far down the street. I considered walking, but because of the snow and slush covering the sidewalk I decided to drive.

The only people in the restaurant were older men, all clustered in the same area. As I stood in line I could hear them grumbling about politicians and social security; cynical about everyone and everything. I got a coffee and sat in a booth on the other side of the restaurant, hoping I could be far enough away that I wouldn't have to think about how depressing life would be in forty years.

After a half hour of listening to them drone on and on, I finally couldn't take it anymore and went back to the apartment. This time I walked in without knocking, and MaryAnn was sitting on the love seat, her legs folded beneath her. There was a mug of coffee in her hand; the mug a gag gift I had given to her as a birthday present during the first year we were together. The sleeping bag and pillow were gone.

I walked into the kitchen and poured myself a cup of coffee, then walked back and sat next to her with a few feet separating us.

She looked at me, a tentative expression on her face. "I'm sorry."

I stared silently at the cup I was holding and gave her a half-hearted shrug.

"What do you want to do?" she asked.

I'll admit it was a little gratifying to hear her choke up. "Do you still love me?" I asked.

She nodded as tears appeared at the corner of each eye and began slowly spilling down her cheeks. "It was a stupid mistake."

"Do you still love me?" I asked again.

She scooted over and put her head on my shoulder, her forehead against my arm. "Of course I love you."

I pulled her close and held her for a long time, conflicting thoughts going through my head. There was no way I could trust her again, but I couldn't imagine her not being a part of my life.

"Do you think we'll ever get past it?" I asked.

"I'll do everything I can to make it up to you."

We had dealt with a lot of emotional issues during our first year together. The guy she dated before me had left her for another woman, and she was my first serious relationship.

"What did I do wrong?" I asked.

"I thought you were just wasting my time," she said, pulling away and wiping a palm over her eyes. "Everybody said so."

"How many people know about what you did?"

She chewed her bottom lip, the thing she always did when she was about to lie. "Nobody knows."

I responded by tilting my head and narrowing my eyes, the look I always gave when I didn't believe her.

"Fine," she sighed. "A couple people at work."

"Is that all?"

"Well, I'm sure there were people in restaurants and places like that," she said with a little attitude. "I didn't go around asking for names."

I nodded and waited a few seconds. "Where did you meet him?"

"Is that important?"

"It must be if you don't want to answer," I said, smiling even though it wasn't heartfelt.

"What difference does it make?"

I rubbed the stubble on the right side of my chin with an index finger. "It might not make any difference at all, but it's going to drive me nuts if I don't know."

"I met him at work, okay?"

She had left the finance company about six months after we met to pursue a career in teaching.

"Does he work there? Is he a parent?"

"He's the gym teacher. And no, he's not married, he's twenty-five, and I think he's a Sagittarius." Saying it like I was being unreasonable.

"I guess that's why you were working late every night," I said, nodding. "That desk of yours must have gotten quite the workout."

"That is absolutely not true," she said, jerking away. "If the school even suspected I'd do something like that, I'd never get another teaching job for the rest of my life."

I got up and took a few steps toward the entertainment center on the opposite side of the room. I knew that if I looked at her I'd probably break down.

"What was it about him that attracted you?" I asked.

"He was just there," she said, almost in a whisper. "First we went out to lunch, just to talk. He listened to me, he didn't push anything. Before I knew it, it just happened."

"So everybody at the school knows about it," I said matter-of-factly.

"Not everybody."

"Trust me. If one of them knows about it, they all know. I work in an office full of women, and not a single one of them can keep their mouths shut about anything, especially something like this."

"What difference does it make?"

"Are you serious? What difference does it make?" I asked, turning to face her. "The difference is that they all must think I'm an idiot."

"They've barely even met you."

"There's also the fact that this is a guy you're going to see every day."

"God, Houston," she said, rolling her eyes. "It's not like we make out behind the bleachers. The reason I asked him to come over last night was so there wouldn't be any confrontation at school on Monday."

I pretended to think about it, even though I'd already made up my mind. "So I guess this means we're back together?"

She nodded, and I leaned over to pick up my coat. The ring was still in the left-hand pocket and I pulled out the box.

"Will you marry me?" I asked.

She put both arms around me. "Of course I'll marry you."

I pulled her left hand from around my neck and slid the ring onto her finger. "I love you," I said, pushing her away a little so I could look into her eyes. "I want you to be with me. Always."

"I love you, too," she whispered. With every fiber of my soul I wanted to believe her.

The next few weeks were equally odd and exciting. Maybe it was my imagination, but when MaryAnn announced our engagement to her friends, family, and various acquaintances I received quite a few peculiar looks. I started to think that more people knew about her cheating than she led on.

It was nice, though, to see bridal magazines on the coffee table, the sofa, everywhere. And MaryAnn really went out of her way to show how much she cared for me. Breakfast in bed, candlelight dinners, she even sent me flowers at work. All we talked about was the wedding. Still, despite her best efforts I could feel a strange emptiness; like there was a hole somewhere between my heart and stomach. Some days I was happy about everything, but there were others that I couldn't get out of bed.

I wanted to confide in someone, but I was too embarrassed to discuss it with my friends and family. The only person left was MaryAnn, but she had no interest in talking about the situation. As far as she was concerned it was in the past.

Around that time, I met a girl in the office named Amber Benson. Every few months, management changes the seating arrangement. My employer says it's because they want to give folks an opportunity for a better shift, but my opinion is that they don't want people getting too comfortable. I guess they equate comfort with a lack of productivity.

Whatever the reason, I found myself seated next to Amber. She was an attractive girl, not beautiful like MaryAnn, but still pretty. She had dark hair, and eyes that could best be described as bewitching. They were slightly tilted and black as midnight. She would look at me and it was hard to make eye contact, but once I did so it was equally difficult to look away. She was dating a guy in the office who played basketball with me, and from what little I knew, he seemed like a nice enough guy.

Things were very casual at first; most of our conversations consisting of "how are you?" and "how was your weekend?" The "how are yous" evolved into emails being sent every fifteen minutes or so, usually stupid things about people in the office or what we'd done over the weekend. That gradually led into taking long walks together during our breaks. At the time, I thought of it simply as a way to pass the time, but the more time we spent together, the more I could see that I was treading on dangerous ground.

It started very innocently on the first sunny day of the year. At the time we had been sitting together for a little less than a month. It was the middle of March, and Amber asked if I wanted to go for a walk during our break.

I asked about her family and she started talking about her mother and father; how they were divorced and she never saw much of her dad. He was an alcoholic who floated in and out of her life. Her mother had remarried and her stepfather had taken over the fatherly responsibilities. It was the first time we discussed anything substantial. Somewhere in the middle of her story, she started to get choked up, and I instinctively reached out and touched her face, then just as quickly drew it back. We looked at each other for a long moment before walking back to the office in silence. We stayed like that once we got to our desks, both of us staring at our computer screens.

I watched her reflection through my monitor, and I saw her turn. "I'm sorry for what happened on the trail," she said. "That's not something I talk about very much."

I faced my computer for another few seconds before turning around. "And I'm sorry for touching you the way I did. I don't know what that was all about."

Her face colored. "I thought it was nice," she said quietly.

"I'm a giver," I said, using the line I was famous for around the office. "My fiancé is always saying I'm too affectionate."

"And Dave is always saying I'm too emotional." Dave, of course, was the guy in the office who she was dating.

"Are you okay now?"

She gave me a tentative shrug, and it was all I could do not to touch her again.

"If there's anything else I can do," I offered.

My imagination started going a little crazy and I found myself fantasizing about us talking at our desks and then we start kissing; making out right there in front of everybody. Our bodies touching, her hair…

"Are you okay?" she asked.

I must have been staring. "I was thinking that if you ever need someone to talk to all you need to do is let me know," I said lamely.

That day marked a new beginning for us. There was a connection, and to be honest it scared me. The next few weeks I steered our conversations back to more general topics; things like the NCAA tournament, music, anything that wasn't on an emotional level.

At home, I could feel MaryAnn drifting away. The initial euphoria of getting engaged had worn off. There was quite a few times where I would catch her looking off into the distance with a melancholy expression. I also noticed that she was rarely around, and she avoided me as much as possible.

As for intimacy, we were going through the motions. I had to face the possibility that MaryAnn and I would break up, and it scared me. I tried to convince myself I would be better off, but in my heart I believed I could never find another girl who could measure up. She was absolutely stunning, beautiful in a way that no other woman I'd dated could compete. So even though I thought our relationship would inevitably fail, I wanted to hang on for as long as I could.

Things went on like that for about a month or so. Around the end of April, I came back from lunch to find Amber hunched over in her chair. I watched her and every few seconds her shoulders would shudder.

"You okay?" I asked.

She looked up at me, teary-eyed, and I reached into my back pocket, took out the handkerchief I always carry and offered it to her.

"Thank you," she said, taking it from my hand.

I turned toward my computer, and then back to her. "You want to go for a walk?" I asked.

She nodded so we walked outside and started down one of the trails. The trees cloaked the path on each side and the limbs canopied overhead blocked out the sun, making it look more like dusk than midday. We walked for at least a couple of minutes in silence. I kept sneaking glances, but she was staring at the ground.

"They put my father in the hospital," she said finally. "The doctors don't know how much time he has left. When my mom told me he was in bad shape, the first thing I could think of is what an asshole he's been."

There was a bench a few feet away and I steered her in that direction. "Is this your real father?" I asked.

She nodded. I had no idea what to say that would be appropriate. "I'm sorry" was too cliché. "Is there anything I can do?" was too generic. "Why did you think that?" was too personal. Instead of saying anything I pulled her close.

"I haven't seen him for over a year," she said, her head against my chest. "The last couple months he's been calling, asking if I want to go out, but I'll either avoid his call or tell him I'm busy."

"I'm sure if you tell Donna, she'll let you take off," I said. Donna was our manager. "If you want, even, I'll take a half-day vacation so I can drive you there."

She looked up at me and touched my cheek with two fingers. Before I realized what was happening, I tilted her head up and we were kissing. After we finally broke apart, my first thoughts drifted to MaryAnn. Would she find out? Would Amber want a relationship?

"I've wanted to do that for a while," she murmured. She looked so small and fragile; almost like a little girl.

"I hope you don't think I was taking advantage of you," I said. "This definitely wasn't what I had in mind when I asked if you wanted to walk."

"I wanted it to happen," she said, pressing her head further against my chest.

I started to feel a little paranoid. There was no telling who would come around the corner and see us entangled. If they did, the news would travel through the office like a plague.

"What about Dave?" I asked.

"I didn't tell you?" she asked, pulling away. "We broke up a few weeks ago. The more I thought about it, he wasn't the right guy for me."

She looked up, a shy smile on her face. "He wasn't like you."

Chapter 3

I was in trouble. A clandestine relationship was one thing, but this was leading into something altogether different. I didn't want to break up with MaryAnn; maybe get even, but not end it.

"Huh," I said, the word coming out sounding like a punctured tire.

It obviously wasn't the reaction she expected. "Is something wrong?" she asked.

I started to say "no," but reconsidered. "Well, yeah. I'm engaged."

"Oh, okay," she said getting to her feet. We started back toward the office, me about a step behind. Her eyes were focused straight ahead, almost like she had tunnel vision.

"I'm sorry about what happened back there," I said, once we were in site of the main entrance.

"It's okay."

"I'll still take that half-day if you want."

"No. I'll be fine." Saying it like I was a stranger offering to carry her groceries.

We got back, and Amber walked directly into our manager's office. She came out a few minutes later, got a few things off her desk, and said a quick goodbye. That was the last I saw of her for about a week and a half.

During that time, things started getting worse between me and MaryAnn. Gone were the bridal magazines and the talks about where we would get married, gone were the candlelight dinners and the breakfasts in bed. The times I did see her she'd say she was busy with one thing or another.

I also noticed that she wouldn't look me in the eye, or make any eye contact at all for that matter. I started to get desperate.

The day Amber returned to work, things were awkward. I was sitting at my desk when she arrived, and she tried to smile at me, but it looked more like she'd eaten some bad Chinese food.

"I missed talking with you," I said after she sat down. "How are things with your dad?"

"They think he'll pull through," she said. I thought there might be something else she wanted to say, but after looking at me for a long moment she turned to face her computer.

"That's great," I said to her back. "Did you get to straighten things out with him?"

She turned slightly, giving me a glimpse of her profile. "I think things will be better from now on."

"Well, that's good."

It was awkward to say the least. For the rest of the week, I pretended to stay busy while she did the same. Most of that time was spent trying to think of a way to salvage my relationship with MaryAnn. I booked a chalet in Gatlinburg for the weekend, figuring the five-hour drive would give us a chance to talk things out.

After much grumbling, MaryAnn agreed to go. I filled a cooler with Stewart's root beer and Starbucks mocha frapuccino which had always been her favorites.

I took a vacation day on Friday to get my stuff together and take care of all the necessary details. I got the oil changed, picked up a silk negligee at Victoria Secret, and bought a bottle of her favorite perfume.

I had planned to leave by six, but MaryAnn didn't walk through the door until after seven. She took her time getting ready, and I could tell she had no interest in going on the trip. Ordinarily, I would have offered to cancel, but I was desperate.

We were out the door around eight and for the first hour or so she had the radio blaring. Several times I tried to turn it down, but she would shoot me an irritated frown before turning it back to the original volume. Finally, I couldn't take it anymore.

"Is something wrong?" I asked, turning off the radio.

She looked out the passenger-side window with her arms crossed. "You mean other than this little power play?"

"What's wrong with trying to have a conversation with my fiancé?"

She rolled her eyes. "Nothing's wrong, Houston."

"If nothing's wrong, why don't you want to talk?"

"Are you saying I need to explain why I don't want to explain? That's about the dumbest thing I've ever heard."

"What is wrong with you?" I asked, raising my voice. "Why don't you ever want to spend time with me anymore?"

"God, Houston. Why does it always have to be about you? School is coming to an end so I have to meet with parents, I have papers to grade. I don't need to hear you whining about being neglected."

Maybe it was my imagination. "If I'm being selfish, it's only because I care about you so much."

"Now you're trying to put me on a guilt trip. Why are you always doing this to me?"

"Doing what? Expecting my fiancé to spend time with me? Or at least pretend like she wants to?"

She gave me a look of defiance, arms crossed tightly, and her chin down against her chest. "There's no easy way to do this," she said. "Pull over at the next exit."

I had a pretty good idea what was about to happen. I pulled into a rest stop, and put the car in idle.

"Okay," I said, more as a question.

She pulled the engagement ring off of her finger and held it out to me. "I don't think we should get married. In fact, I think we should break up."

I stared at the ring in her hand and started to reach for it, but stopped. "Is there someone else?"

She sighed and rolled her eyes. "Does it matter?"

"Hell yeah, it matters. Less than two months ago you swore you'd never cheat on me again."

"Do you really want to do this to yourself?"

I nodded. "I really do."

"Fine. Kevin said he wants to get back together."

It took me a few seconds to realize who she was talking about. "You mean the same Kevin who dumped you before we started dating?"

She didn't say anything, just stared impatiently out the window.

"Let me see if I understand," I said, talking slowly. "The guy breaks your heart, dumps you for a stripper, refuses to talk to you other than to say you mean nothing to him, then out of the blue he calls and you take him back? And this after you beg and plead for me to forgive you?"

"Don't make this worse than it has to be."

"Please explain to me how it can get worse."

"What difference does it make who it is?"

I raised my eyebrows and shrugged. "Maybe none, but when he dumps you again don't come crying to me."

"I'm not happy with you," she said, looking at me like I was supposed to understand. "If it wasn't him it would have been someone else."

I jerked my head back. "What's that supposed to mean?"

"Ever since you found out I cheated on you, you've acted like I should wear a scarlet "A" on my chest. You think I want to go through that the rest of my life?"

"How can you say that?" I asked, gesturing wildly. "If anything, I've acted like it never happened."

"It doesn't make a difference. There's nothing you can do about it anyway."

"How about I make you walk your ass back to Cincinnati?"

She put my ring on the dashboard. "If that makes you feel better."

I got out of the car and pulled her gym bag from the trunk. Once I placed in on the sidewalk I got back in.

"And the apartment is mine," I said.

"You're so immature."

I pointed to her bag. "You might want to get that."

She slammed the door and picked up her bag. As she turned, I thought about how ironic it was that even now I was completely mesmerized watching her walk away.

I sat for a minute or so with the car in idle before turning off the ignition. After contemplating a little longer, I got out of the car and went after her. She was talking on her cell phone when I caught up.

"There's no reason for you to sit here and wait for someone," I said. "Get in the car."

She narrowed her eyes and chewed her lip, pretending to consider my offer. "Thank you," she said, still with the attitude.

She put her bag back in the trunk. "There's Stewies and fraps in the cooler if you want one," I said once she was in the passenger seat.

She reached back and opened the cooler. "Get me one, too, if you don't mind," I said. She pulled out two root beers and after twisting off the caps, put one on my side of the beverage holder.

"It'll take me a few days to find a place," I said.

She seemed to consider it. "Of course I'll sleep on the couch," I added.

"Are you going to give me money for rent this month?"

It shocked me how nonchalant she was about the whole thing. "I guess, whatever you think is fair," I said.

Those were the last words we exchanged during the trip home. The first thing I did when we walked through the door was call the chalet and cancel my reservation. Even though I lied and said it was because my mother was in the hospital, they made me pay for the full night on Friday, and half for Saturday and Sunday.

Next, I called my brother, Rob, and asked if I could stay at his place until I got settled. That led into a conversation about why I needed a place to stay, which led to me telling him that it was none of his business. After telling me that I was a presumptuous prick, he agreed to let me move in as soon as I could get everything together.

Rob lived in a large one-bedroom apartment in what could best be described as a colorful part of town. In the few months he'd lived there, his car had been broken into twice. Needless to say I hoped my stay would be a short one.

Once I was off the phone, I started packing my stuff into boxes. Somewhere between getting everything from the closet and carrying it to the car, it hit home that MaryAnn was breaking up with me. And not for anything I had done, but instead to be with someone else, someone she had claimed to despise. It took everything I could muster not to sit in the middle of the room and dissolve in a puddle of tears. That night I didn't sleep a wink.

I started bringing everything over to my brother's apartment the next morning, and by Sunday, I was completely moved in. There wasn't room for any of my stuff in his drawers, so I left it in boxes. The sofa had a hideaway bed, and my brother gave me the option of either sleeping there or on the floor.

At some point Sunday afternoon I passed out. I woke up around three in the morning thinking about playing cards with MaryAnn and couldn't go back to sleep. I rolled around for a while before I finally got up and stumbled toward the kitchen.

Everything was dark and since I didn't know the apartment all that well, I bumped into three or four things on my way. I figured Rob would wake up, but as far as I could tell he didn't stir. I inventoried his liquor cabinet and found a half-empty fifth of Bacardi Light Rum, and maybe a finger of Jack Daniels. I went through his cabinets until I got to the one with cups, took out the biggest I could find, and then rummaged through the refrigerator.

I took out a two-liter bottle of Pepsi and filled the cup about half full, added some ice cubes from the freezer, and poured in seven or eight ounces of rum. After taking a sip that burned my throat, I got a spoon out of the sink, turned it handle up and stirred my drink.

As I sat staring at the ceiling and drinking my Bacardi and Pepsi, I replayed in my mind all I could of my relationship with MaryAnn: the time I met her at work, our first date when I had to borrow my sister's car, our long walks, drinking wine and making love by candlelight.

Along with the good things, of course, were the bad: the moment I realized she'd cheated on me, the look on her face when she broke up with me, watching her put my ring on the dashboard. I tried to convince myself that I was better off, but I still loved her. Not only that, but I was alone for the first time in three years.

I tried to go back to sleep after finishing my drink, but I was restless. By the time I got drowsy again, I had to pee. I fought the urge for at least an hour, but finally made my way to the bathroom. After that, I couldn't sleep. I watched the clock make its slow crawl and went to the bathroom every hour or so. I was somewhere between asleep and awake when I heard my brother's alarm go off. I sat up in bed and watched him stagger out of his room.

"You sleep all right?" he asked.

"You know how it is," I said, stretching. "You getting in the shower first, or should I?"

He grinned. "There's only so much hot water. Good luck."

As soon as he was out of sight, I reached over and pulled a pair of khakis out of a box and put them on over my boxers. My shirts and socks were in another box, and I had to get up to find them. About twenty minutes later my brother came out of the bathroom, clad only in a towel.

"Don't turn either of the knobs too far. You do, you'll have a hell of a time adjusting the temperature."

I could hear him slamming things around in his bedroom as I got in the shower. About halfway through rinsing the shampoo from my hair, the hot water was gone. One good thing about the cold water, though, was it helped wake me up.

I got out of the shower, and as I brushed my teeth I found myself thinking about Amber. What would be the right time to tell her that MaryAnn and I had broke up? Right away? Kind of slip it into conversation?

Amber hadn't arrived when I got to work, so I walked down to the cafeteria and got us both a cup of coffee. She was sitting at her desk when I got back to my cubicle.

"I got you a coffee, two cream, three sugars" I said, placing the cup in front of her. I thought maybe she'd be impressed that I remembered how she took it, but no such luck.

"Thank you," she said, avoiding my eyes. I guess I shouldn't have expected much conversation after the way we'd been avoiding one another.

We had about ten minutes before our shift started, and I decided to take the big plunge. "I've been thinking a lot lately about what happened between us on the trail a few weeks ago."

"At the time I was upset," she said in a clipped tone. "I'm sorry if I offended you."

"No, you didn't offend me," I said quickly. "Actually, it got me thinking. I really have a good time with you, and I'd like to see you. Outside of work, I mean."

"What about your fiancé?" she asked, turning to face me.

I waived my hand like I was shooing a fly. "That's over."

"When did you break up?"

Things weren't progressing nearly as well as I'd hoped. "It's been happening for a while now."

She tapped her long manicured fingernails on her desk. "Right now I'm kind of seeing a guy."

I'm sure my face turned the same deep red as her nail polish. "Bad luck then," I said, turning to face my computer.

I kicked myself for not asking if she was seeing someone before I made an ass of myself. After about an hour of pretending to work, I finally summoned the nerve to turn back around.

"I didn't just make things awkward, did I?"

She turned. "No more than I did that day on the trail."

We sat staring at each other, both wearing expressions that weren't quite smiles, but close enough.

"What I was trying to say before I stuck my foot in my mouth is that I think you're a great girl… woman… person, whatever. My point is that I want to go out with you. I should have asked if you had a boyfriend before I did, though."

I saw the nosy woman who sits across the partition from Amber peer over. She made eye contact, and I gave her a dirty look. Her head quickly disappeared.

"I'm sorry," I said, lowering my tone.

"I didn't say I had a boyfriend."

If I looked confused, there was a good reason. "Huh?"

"You said you didn't know I had a boyfriend."

"I thought…"

"Look," she interrupted. "It's no secret I like you, but I don't want to be your rebound girl, or the girl you use to get back with your fiancé, or whatever."

"I told you. Me and her are through."

"Let me finish," she said, looking at me expectantly. "As I was saying, I've already dated one guy I work with, and I swore that I'd never do it again."

"I guess that's a real no, then."

She hesitated before nodding. "How about walks?" I asked. "Are those off limits, too?"

"We'll see."

"How about now? Just as friends."

She laughed. "We have to wait 'til our next break."

"I say we're adults and we can take our break whenever we want."

She grabbed her badge and we headed out the door. After we'd walked in silence for several minutes, I looked behind to make sure no one was there and came to a stop. She took a few more steps, and then turned around.

"Is something wrong?" she asked.

I moved toward her until there were only a few inches separating us. "I don't care that we work together. I don't care what people in the office think. Right now, I don't even care if you have a boyfriend."

I tilted up her chin with an index finger. "I can't stop thinking about you," I said. "Here at work, the only thing I do all day is stare at the reflection of the back of your head through my monitor."

She stood on her tiptoes and I leaned down to kiss her. In the few seconds our lips were connected I forgot about the whole thing with MaryAnn. After Amber and I broke apart, she smiled and touched my cheek.

"I stare at you, too," she said.

Chapter 4

"Is Dave still a friend of yours?" she asked after we'd gotten back to our desks. Dave was the guy in the office who she had previously dated. "I don't know that I ever considered him a friend exactly. We play ball together, but that's about it."

"When I broke up with him, he asked if it was so I could go out with you."

I thought back on it. "I remember around the time you two broke up, he asked if I had a girlfriend. It weirded me out because I didn't know him all that well."

"Will that bother you?"

"You mean him finding out?" I asked, and she nodded. "Like I said, we're not friends. I could care less what he thinks."

"Do you think he will?"

"I saw Margaret stand up and look over when I asked you out, so I'm sure everyone in the office knows by now."

Margaret was the nosy woman who had listened in on our conversation. "I guess it doesn't matter," she said. "Everyone already thinks we're sleeping together."

The next few days were a blast. We spent the days at work flirting back and forth, kind of getting to know one another. There was a lot we already knew, but it was different when there was an element of intimacy involved.

MaryAnn still hadn't called, and I hadn't heard from her since the day I'd packed my boxes. I had tried to privatize my number and call her, but there was a message saying the number I was dialing wouldn't accept blocked calls. More than once I had to fight the urge to drive past the apartment.

I hadn't lived with my brother since I'd moved in with MaryAnn so we were getting re-acquainted. Back in the old days, we were living in a cramped two-bedroom apartment in a nice area. Here, the apartment was nicer, but the neighbors left something to be desired.

I got home around 5:30 on a Tuesday afternoon, and Rob was sprawled out on the couch watching TV. "MaryAnn called a few minutes ago," he said.

"Yeah?" I asked, trying to sound casual about it. "She say what she wants?"

"Just said to call her at home." He smirked. "Maybe you won't be here as long as you thought."

"We're through," I said. "You mind if I take it in your room?"

He motioned that way, keeping his eyes on the television. I walked into his room and sat on the bed. For a long time I stared at the phone, not sure if I should call or not. Well, that's not true. I was wondering if calling her was a mistake. Even though I knew I'd call her eventually, I was trying to talk myself into staying calm.

It was useless. I dialed the first six numbers fairly quickly; on the last digit I had my hand poised over the number for a long moment. I couldn't do it, at least not yet. I turned it off and walked back out into the living room.

"That was quick," my brother said.

"Funny guy," I said, grabbing a beer out of the refrigerator.

"Hey sensuous," he said, holding up his empty can. I didn't even change expression as I got another beer and carried it over. My brother thought it was hilarious to say "Hey sensuous" and when the person said what, he'd say "sensuous up, grab me a beer," or a piece of pizza, or whatever else he happened to want at that moment. I took a long drink and walked back into Rob's room carrying the phone. Before I could chicken out, I quickly dialed MaryAnn's number, my old number. She answered on the second ring.

"Hey," I said.

"Can I call you back later?" she asked, sounding agitated.

"What are you pissed off for? You called me."

"Houston, I need to call you back," she said. I started to respond, but then heard the click and shortly thereafter a dial tone.

I stared at the phone with mixed emotions. Hearing her voice when she said hello was almost like a new beginning. How could such an insignificant have such a profound effect? Then after the hello, I got the same attitude she'd given me during our final weeks together.

I sat back down on the bed and called Amber. "Hey, you busy?" I asked when she answered.

"Actually, my dad's on the other line."

"Can you give me a call after you're done?"

She hesitated. "Okay. I don't know how long it'll be, though."

"Take your time."

I walked back into the living room and put the phone back on the charger. My brother hadn't moved from where he was sitting.

"You on your way out the door?" he asked.

"I told you, man. We're through. How many more times you want me to say it?"

"Touchy, touchy," he said, putting his palms out. "While you're up, you mind grabbing me another one?"

I got another beer out of the refrigerator and sat next to him on the couch. "If MaryAnn calls again tell her I'm not here."

He finally moved a little, turning his body toward me. "You think she's going to call?"

I shrugged. "I'm only saying if she does."

"You got some other girl lined up?"

"Something like that."

He slapped me on the leg. "She a hottie?"

"She's not as pretty as MaryAnn, but yeah, she's pretty."

He snickered and looked back at the television. "That's trouble. 'Not as pretty as MaryAnn,'" he mimicked.

"I'm just saying she's not as pretty. Just like Mom always says you're not as smart as me. That doesn't mean you're an idiot."

"Mom never said that."

I took a last swallow of my beer before tossing it toward the garbage can. "Maybe not to you."

"You're an ass," he muttered.

I got another beer from the fridge. "God, can't you take a joke? Okay, fine. Mom never said it."

He glared up at me for a few seconds. "That doesn't mean it's any less true," I said.

The phone rang and I looked over at him expectantly.

"You're so smart, figure out who's on the phone," he said, not moving. I started over to the phone but stopped.

"You going to answer that?" he asked.

"It's not my house," I said.

He had the same goofy message that was in the movie "Big Daddy." It was the chorus to the song "Jump" by Van Halen, except when the song said "Might as well jump," he replaced the jump with "leave a message." My brother was an idiot.

"Hi, Houston, it's MaryAnn. If you're there, please pick up the phone."

I looked over at my brother, knowing that if I did I'd never hear the end of it.

"Fine," she continued. "When you get this message give me a call. I have some of your mail, and there are still a few things we need to talk about."

"I guess I should call her back," I said to my brother, trying to sound resigned to it.

He snickered and took another swallow of his beer. "You're a real hard ass," he said.

I went over and picked up the phone. "You know what you might want to do," he said. "Give her a call and tell her you wanted to let her know you're not in."

I ignored him and dialed her number. She answered after the first ring.

"Hey," I said, much more subdued than the time before.

"Sorry about earlier. How are you holding up?"

I gave a sideways glance at my brother as I walked into the bathroom, and then turned on the fan. "Okay, I guess. My brother's an even worse slob than the last time we lived together, but other than that…"

"Do you think you'll be able to stop by?"

I checked out my reflection in the mirror and patted a few stray hairs into place. "You mean right now?"

"If you're not busy."

"No," I said, checking my teeth. "Give me fifteen minutes."

"Can you bring a check for this month's rent when you come?"

"How much should I make it out for?" I asked, giving it a little attitude.

"There's other stuff I want to talk about, too," she said defensively.

I hung up the phone and grabbed my keys off the counter. "I'm getting my mail from MaryAnn."

"I think you're forgetting something," he said.

I was halfway out the door and stopped. "Huh?"

"You left your pink panties with the cute little bow on the front in the bathroom," he said, pointing in that direction.

I gave him a deadpan stare. "Funny guy," I said, closing the door behind me.

It was almost 6:30, so traffic was light. The distance to MaryAnn's was about five miles, and I made it there in a less than ten minutes. MaryAnn opened the door wearing a little t-shirt that showed her belly and a tight pair of shorts that had the waistband rolled up so that it was just below her butt. I put as much effort as I could muster into appearing unaffected.

"You said you had some mail," I said, looking past her.

I could tell it wasn't the reaction she expected. She disappeared into the bedroom, and brought back a small stack.

"And you wanted me to bring a check," I said, more as a question.

She looked up at me over her lashes; something she knew turned me on. "Can I get you something to drink?"

I looked down at my non-existent watch. "I'm kind of in a hurry," I said.

"Can't you sit and talk for five minutes with an old friend?"

I pretended to consider it, and then took a seat on the couch. "Okay, I guess I'll take a glass of water."

She walked into the kitchen and filled a cup with water from the faucet. "I know you only stayed for a few days this month, so just give me what you think is fair."

"Is a hundred okay?"

"That's fine," she said, carrying over the glass and setting it on a coaster.

I filled out the check and set it on the end table next to the couch. "You need anything else?" I asked.

"I'm sorry about what happened," she said, clasping her hands like she was in prayer.

I tried to keep a straight face. "Haven't we had this conversation before?"

"I'm not asking to get back together," she said, rolling her eyes. "I just miss talking to you."

"Oh, yeah? The way I remember it, the last few weeks we were together you didn't do much talking at all. Well, unless we're counting the time you broke up with me again."

She put her face in her hands. "I was confused, okay?"

"I have to go," I said, getting off the couch. I hadn't realized how mad and hurt I was until that moment. It felt like she was cutting out my heart with a spoon.

I had my hand on the doorknob when she said, "Kevin and I aren't seeing each other anymore."

I stopped and turned around. "Yeah?"

There were tears in her eyes. "He's going back to his old girlfriend."

"What do you want me to do about it?"

"I can't believe I was so stupid," she said, putting her arms around me. I kept my hands at my sides, fighting the urge to hold her.

"I'm not playing the fool again," I said. "This one you need to work out on your own."

"Three years together and that's all you have to say?"

"What do you want me to say, MaryAnn? Do you want me to tell you to keep your head up? Do you want me to say that sometimes bad things happen to good people? You broke my heart not once, but twice. You expect me to be sympathetic?"

"I thought we could just sit down and talk," she said, turning away.

I sat down on the couch. "You want to talk, MaryAnn? Come on over here and we'll talk."

I patted the cushion next to the one I was on. "What do you want to talk about? Global warming? The financial crisis? The two times you cheated on me? The two times you dumped me? Talk away, sweetheart."

"Do you think this is funny?" she asked, turning to face me.

The look on her face made me feel a little guilty. "I'm sorry," I said. There was a little mascara at the corner of her right eye, and I brushed away off with an index finger. Less than five minutes later we were in bed and she was un-zipping my pants. I felt completely out of control, like I was stuck in some bizarre dream. I wanted to tell her that it wasn't right; that I wasn't a yo-yo or some kind of puppy dog, but instead, I let it happen.

After it was over, I felt empty. There was no way that we could ever get back together; there was no way I'd ever be able to get her out of my mind. I was lying next to her, staring at the ceiling, and I started crying.

The sobs came in big, rolling heaves. The more I tried to stop, the harder they came. I could see MaryAnn staring at me like I was some kind of zoo exhibit, but there was nothing I could do. It took several minutes to compose myself.

"Are you okay?"

I took a deep breath and nodded. "Just confused."

She was still lying beside me, the blanket covering just above her waist. "If it helps any, I'm confused, too."

"What does this mean, exactly?"

"It doesn't have to mean anything," she said, putting her head on my shoulder.

I sat up so I could look over at her. "That's the thing. I know we can't get back together. I know that. No matter how much I love you, no matter how much I think about you, no matter how much I miss you, it won't work."

"What do you want to do?"

I rolled over on top of her and looked into her eyes. "I want to make love to you one more time. After that, I never want to see you again."

We made love, never once breaking eye contact. Every emotion I could feel ran through me. I forgot about everything else, and tried to remember every detail of her face; the exact color of her eyes. I wanted that image burned into my brain. It was the single most erotic moment of my life. After it was over, I willed myself out of bed and got dressed.

"Why can't you see me anymore?" she asked, completely uncovered.

"If I see you, it takes everything inside me not to touch you. I'm not putting myself through that anymore."

I leaned over and kissed her on the cheek. "Goodbye, MaryAnn."

She didn't say anything, and I assumed she was still lying in bed when I walked out the door. It wasn't until after I started my car and was on my way to my brother's that I thought of Amber. God, I was such an ass. The more I thought about it, the more I realized I was doing the same thing MaryAnn had done to me.

Cars flew past, their lights a blur. I pulled into the complex and was on my way into the apartment when a voice stopped me.

"I tried to call you three or four times." I closed my eyes and turned to face Amber.

Chapter 5

"I had to drop off a check. Is everything okay with your dad?" I asked, a shameless attempt to change the subject.

"Nothing's changed," she said, walking over and giving me a hug. "I was worried about you."

"Yeah?"

"We can go out to a restaurant or something if you want," she said, looking at me expectantly.

More than anything I wanted a shower. "I would, but I have a killer headache," I said, rubbing my temples. "If my brother's place wasn't such a wreck, I'd invite you in."

"Actually, your brother invited me to come wait for you. He said you were taking care of some business, but you said to just meet you here. He even gave me directions."

"He did, huh?" I asked, wanting to strangle him. "He's always so helpful."

I opened the apartment door. "Just want to warn you, the place looks like the fifth ring of hell." I said. "Don't expect much."

Rob was in the same position he had been when I left. I made the introductions and Rob looked up at me with a sly grin. "You were right, brother. She's a very beautiful girl."

"You said that?" she asked, sounding flattered.

"Yeah," I said, glancing over at my brother, and then back at Amber. "You want a beer or something?"

"I'll take one," my brother said. I kept looking at Amber and she finally nodded. There were only three beers left, so I grabbed them and carried them into the living room.

"How did your business venture work out?" my brother asked.

I dropped the beer in his lap. "Sorry about that. It went fine."

"So Houston tells me that you work together," he said to Amber, placing the beer unopened on the lamp stand. "Are all the girls there as pretty as you?"

Amber forced a smile and gave me a sideways glance. "Well…"

"You'll have to excuse my brother," I said, patting her on the knee. "At the pawn shop where he works, he doesn't get the chance to see many attractive women."

The look on his face showed I'd struck a blow. "That pawn shop is the reason you have a roof over your head."

"All I'm saying is there aren't many good-looking women," I said innocently.

He and I stared each other down for a few moments, and I finally turned to Amber. "On second thought, my head's feeling better," I said.

Amber looked at my brother and then at me. "Okay."

She turned back to Rob. "It was nice to meet you. Thanks for what you said on the phone."

The prick. I didn't even look in his direction as we walked out the door.

"We can take my car," she offered. I climbed in the passenger seat and we drove to the McDonalds about a block away. She got an ice cream, and I ordered a Sprite and a large fry.

"So what was that all about?" she asked.

"What do you mean?"

"I'm not stupid. There was something going on between you two," she said, pretending to keep it casual while she licked her ice cream.

I thought about lying, but changed my mind. "My ex-girlfriend had some of my mail, and I also needed to drop off a check for the money I owed her."

"Is that all?"

"She wanted to hash out all the details about who gets what. I think that's why I had a headache."

"Did you tell her about me?"

"I told her I was seeing someone, but I don't know if I mentioned your name." It was kind of true. I vaguely remembered saying something about seeing a girl.

She stopped eating her ice cream. "Do you want to get back with her?"

I took a long drink of my Sprite to buy a little time. "I think after you get engaged, if you break up there's no going back. What's the point?"

"Am I the girl you want to be with?"

"Of course you are," I said, trying not to sound patronizing.

"Because I don't want to start a relationship with you if I have to wonder if the only reason you're seeing me is so I can take the place of your ex-girlfriend."

"I don't blame you."

She smiled, and I leaned across the table to give her a kiss. "We could head back to my place for a nightcap if you want," she offered.

I knew there was no way I could pull that off without her knowing about what happened between me and MaryAnn. "You have no idea how much I'd like to do that, but I can't. How about I take a rain check for tomorrow night?"

I could tell that wasn't the response she'd expected. "Do you want me to take you back to your brother's?" she asked.

I nodded and we headed back. Once we pulled into the parking lot I gave her a long kiss goodbye and got out.

My brother wasn't sitting on the couch, and I was getting ready to send out a search party when I heard the toilet flush. A couple seconds later he came out carrying the phone.

"MaryAnn called. She said to give her a call back no what time you got in," he said.

"MaryAnn's out of luck," I said, walking to the fridge. I looked inside. "And you're out of beer."

"So how did it go?"

I looked over at him without saying anything. "What? I can't ask a simple question?"

"It went fine, both with MaryAnn and with Amber."

"Uh huh," he said with a grin. "I know the way a woman sounds when she's gotten that loving feeling."

"What's your point?"

"Come on, brother. I ain't stupid."

"I'll tell you one more time," I said, turning toward him. "Things are over between me and MaryAnn. Over, finis, done."

"You're sure about that?"

"Am I using the big words again? I said I'm sure."

There was a brief pause, and I thought for a moment that he would drop the subject. "Are you going to let me smell your fingers?" he asked.

I rolled my eyes. "You need help."

"No," he said, trying to look serious. "Purely for scientific purposes."

"The only thing my fingers smell like is french fries. I'm going to bed."

Another pause. "Amber seems like a nice girl. You're not going to dick her around, are you?"

"So what if I am?" I asked, pulling out the couch and grabbing my blanket from a pile in the hallway closet.

"Did you sleep with MaryAnn tonight?"

"Jesus," I said, raising my voice a little. "What's with the twenty questions? Don't worry about it. To set the record straight, MaryAnn and I will never date again. I'll probably go out with Amber, but I'm not sure right now. End of conversation. I don't want to hear about it anymore."

It was silent as I stripped down to my boxers and lay down. "Do you think you can pick up a twelve-pack?" he asked not long after I'd closed my eyes.

"I'll do it tomorrow," I grumbled.

There was another period of silence and I was almost asleep when my brother asked, "Does Amber have a sister?"

"I don't know," I said, opening my eyes long enough to glare at him. "If you leave me alone for the rest of the night, I'll ask."

He muttered something about me being an ungrateful prick as he turned off the living room light and went back to bed. Even though there was a lot on my mind I was asleep almost immediately.

I was in the middle of a dream where I was in a fight with a guy who I hated in high school when the phone woke me up. Pissed me off because I was really beating the crap out of him.

After the obligatory four rings and my brother's goofy answering machine message, I heard MaryAnn asking where I was and wondering if I was okay. I briefly considered answering it, but knew that if I did I'd never get back to sleep. She said a few more things about our night together and how much she missed me, but at the time I didn't know if I was hearing it, or still dreaming.

Morning came way too soon. I heard Rob's alarm go off, but just as quickly fell back to sleep. I vaguely remembered hearing the shower running, and it seemed like a long time afterward that I was hearing MaryAnn's message again. I looked up to see my brother standing next to the answering machine.

After the message was over he looked at me with a big smirk. "Obviously it's over. I don't know why I didn't believe you."

I put the pillow over my head. "Did you leave me any hot water?"

"No hot water. Sorry. Do you mind if I save this message?"

"God, Rob," I groaned. "Can you just leave it alone?"

He laughed and pressed the play button on the answering machine one more time. I got up and walked into the bathroom, acting more pissed off than I really was. The hot water lasted a little longer this time, but I still ended up rinsing off with cold water. After I brushed my teeth, I walked out into the living room and was met by my brother.

"You want some breakfast?" he asked, his way of apologizing.

I waved him off. "Sorry about that whole thing. I'm just working it all out in my head right now."

I put on my clothes and about ten minutes later was on my way to work. Amber was sitting at her desk when I arrived, and there was a hot cup of coffee next to my keyboard. Neither of us brought up what had happened the previous night. She acted like there was something holding her back, and I could tell that the incident at McDonalds had made her uncomfortable. Honestly, I wasn't entirely comfortable either. The ordeal with MaryAnn was far from being worked out, and I felt a little guilty about what I'd done. Not the sex part because Amber and I weren't official, but there was no doubt in my mind that if Amber found out what had happened she'd never speak to me again.

On our walk that afternoon I almost slipped up and called her MaryAnn, but caught myself just in time. We discussed going out right after work or going home, changing, and then meeting up later. We decided on the latter. Even though I was with Amber all day talking, flirting, and occasional touches that went beyond the boundaries of friendship; through all of that I couldn't stop thinking about MaryAnn and how magical those last few minutes had been; looking into each other's eyes, the connection, the passion. I found myself staring into the distance more than once. I knew I'd said that I never wanted to see her again, but that was impractical if not impossible.

I drove home fully intending to change and drive over to Amber's place. MaryAnn, though, was sitting on the front steps leading into my brother's apartment when I arrived. I saw her almost immediately after turning onto the street, and she got up to meet me when I stepped out of the car.

"Hey," I said.

She looked at me expectantly. "I waited up for you last night."

"Sorry about that," I said, avoiding eye contact.

"I was thinking about what you said, how we shouldn't see each other anymore. I think it's a good idea."

"Then what are you doing here?"

She smiled. "I always like to do what I'm not supposed to."

"Look, MaryAnn. I need to get you out of my head, but that's hard to do when I see you all the time."

She looked at me over long lashes. "You want to kiss me, don't you."

I had to bite my lip to keep from saying yes. "There's somewhere I need to be."

I tried to push past her, but she grabbed my arm, and pulled close. "You want to make love to me, don't you," she murmured in my ear.

My thoughts went back to Amber. "I have to make a quick call," I said.

I walked up the stairs, holding her hand until we were stretched out like a tightrope. I finally pulled away and went into the apartment, closing the door behind me. I grabbed the phone off of the charger and dialed Amber's number trying to think of something to say. I still hadn't figured it out when she answered.

"Are you on your way?" she asked.

"No," I said, racking my brain. "Actually, my mom has the flu and she asked that I come see her."

Almost as soon as the words came out of my mouth, I slapped my forehead with the palm of my hand.

"Do you want me to come with you?"

"No, no," I said, eyes closed. "Hopefully I won't be long. I'll call you when I get back."

"Okay," she said, obviously disappointed. "Tell your mom I hope she feels better."

"I will," I said, and then after a few seconds, "sorry about this."

"No, that's okay."

Upon hanging up, I slapped my head several more times. Of all the stupid things I could come up with. I also felt incredibly guilty. Maybe it would be better to tell MaryAnn that I had another commitment. Hell, I'd already rehearsed the line that my mom was sick.

That was all forgotten when I walked out and saw her leaning against my car. She had her sunglasses on and her shirtsleeves rolled up just above her shoulders. I stood in place staring at her until she smiled at me.

"You driving or me?" I asked.

She pointed to herself. After she unlocked the door I looked over. "Where are we going?" I asked.

"Our place."

"Our place," I thought. I had stopped thinking of it in those terms the day I moved out. The scenery flew by, and I started feeling a little nervous. The way things were developing, we'd be back together. That idea appealed to me on many different levels, but I knew it would never work. She'd already made a fool of me. Not once, but twice. For her I was just a stopgap, someone to play with until the next thing came along. I wasn't complaining, but at the same time I would never get over her at this rate.

We arrived at her apartment -- our apartment -- and there was a bottle of red wine sitting open on the counter. Obviously she'd considered me coming to her place a foregone conclusion.

She kissed me and gently pushed me onto the couch, then went around lighting the candles that decorated the apartment. Once that was done, she poured us both a glass of wine.

"To new beginnings," she said, holding up her glass.

I hesitated before touching mine to hers. "And to old flames."

She smiled, and we lay on the couch together. Neither of us said much, we just lay there touching and kissing. A couple times she got up to refill our glasses. Almost the entire bottle was gone when we made our way back to the bedroom.

Once the act was done I looked down, her head on my chest, and wondered how I could have ever thought that another girl could take her place. We walked out into the living room a few minutes later and drank a little more wine. We both agreed that we were both too drunk to drive so a couple hours later I had a cab pick me up.

"I love you," she whispered when we were saying goodbye. It was the first time she'd said that since the few weeks proceeding our engagement.

The cab ride home was spent in reflection. Should I tell Amber the truth? Should I avoid MaryAnn? Would it be possible to play both sides against the middle without getting caught?

I walked into the apartment, and my brother was in his customary spot on the couch. The Reds were playing St. Louis, and I sat down to watch the game.

"You pick up the beer?" he asked.

I rubbed my eyes with the thumb and forefinger of my left hand. "Shoot. I forgot."

He muttered under his breath and started putting on his shoes. I pulled out my wallet and handed him a twenty, which improved him mood, but not by much.

"You want anything from the store?" he asked.

"Maybe some pretzels."

I sat watching the game, and he returned about fifteen minutes later carrying two cases of Miller Light with a bag of pretzels balanced on top. I took one of the cases he was holding and put it in the fridge.

"You want one?" he asked, opening the case in his hand.

I shook my head. "Drank too much wine earlier."

I moved over a little so he could sit down. "You go out with Amber?"

I looked over at him, but his eyes were focused on the game. "I learned my lesson about telling you anything."

"I was just playing around. It wasn't a big deal."

"You don't think so? I had to answer a lot of questions, and Amber was pissed."

"God, you're touchy. Sorry," he said, drawing out the "sorry."

I shrugged and went back to watching the game. "So did you go out with Amber?" he asked again.

"You going to keep your mouth shut?" I asked, and he nodded. "I went over to MaryAnn's."

Then I remembered what I'd told Amber. "Shoot," I said. "I was supposed to call Amber when I got in. If she asks, I went over to Mom's because she was sick."

Rob made a show of almost spilling his beer. "I tell you what, bro. You keep this up and I won't charge you rent."

"Funny guy," I muttered, taking the phone into the bathroom.

"How's your mom?" Amber asked once she answered the phone.

"She has the flu, but the doctor said she'll be okay," I said, cringing again.

"It's only eight. Do you want to come over?"

I looked at the shower, wondering how long it would take me to clean up, not to mention sober up. Then I'd have to drive the ten to fifteen miles to where she lived. "Sure, give me an hour?"

"See you then."

I quickly undressed, got a towel from the closet and got in the shower. I turned the cold water on full blast hoping that would help sober me up. After I brushed my teeth, I put on a pair of sweats and a t-shirt.

"Where are you going?" my brother asked.

"Amber's," I said, looking for my keys.

He laughed. "You are such a prick."

"Have you seen my keys?"

I walked back to the bathroom where I'd taken off my pants and got them for my left front pocket.

"You okay to drive?" my brother asked.

"Don't worry about it, I'm straight."

"Speaking of straight," he said, "either you're still stuffing your jockeys or you got a souvenir from your get together with MaryAnn."

I looked down, and zipped up my pants. "What's with the vested interest in my love life?" I asked. "You ever think of getting one of your own, or are you going to stick to those special websites?"

"Don't do anything I wouldn't do," he called after me as I walked out.

I got to Amber's about twenty minutes later, ten minutes earlier than my original estimate. She was sitting on the floor and was holding two beers, tops off.

"Come on in," she said, getting to her feet. "I'll give you a tour."

It was a medium sized two-bedroom. "You live here by yourself?"

"I had a roommate, but she moved to Columbus."

"This is nice," I said, looking around. "A lot better than my brother's place."

We walked through the kitchen and then back into the living room. I could see her eyeing me a little, and I had a feeling what was about to happen.

"Let me show you the bedroom," she said, taking my hand. The bed was a queen-size, very stylish four-poster bed. There were teddy bears lying on her bed, her dresser, on the floor, everywhere. Other than the bears, it was spotless.

"Do you have a hard time affording this on your own?"

Her face colored. "My mom and step-dad help me out."

"Nothing wrong with that." We walked out to the living room and she handed me a beer. I relegated myself to being sick since I couldn't tell her that I'd had too much wine at my mom's house.

"I've been thinking about you and me," she said. "Us."

"Yeah?"

"I don't want to pressure you or anything like that, but I think we're starting something."

I reached over and touched her hand. "Me, too."

"The thing I want to know is if you're still seeing your ex-girlfriend, or ex-fiancé, or whatever she is. If you are, just tell me."

The guilt hit me like a tidal wave. "I told you," I said gently. "Me and her are through."

She relaxed. "I'm sorry to bring it up again, but I'd rather find out now than later. I hope I didn't offend you."

I kissed her on the cheek. "Not at all. In your place I'd feel the same way."

She put her arms around me, and I looked skyward. My brother was right. I was definitely a prick. Right then and there I made a vow: no matter how many times MaryAnn called, came over, tried to find me; no matter what, I'd never do anything with her again.

Amber kissed me, first softly and then with a lot more intensity. We went on like that for about ten minutes before I picked her up and carried her back to the bedroom. I had forgotten to bring a condom, but she didn't seem to mind so I didn't make an issue out of it. Things were awkward at the beginning, her trying too hard to please me and vice versa.

After the first few minutes, we found a rhythm. Amber kept trying to look into my eyes, but I had to look away. Maybe ten minutes after we finished we did it again, this time with her on top. There was no looking away this time, and that was probably the worst I ever thought about myself. Guys who did this kind of stuff to women were why so many of them hated men. Somewhere out there was a support group, and I was justifying every negative thing they said.

When it was over she wrapped herself in my arms like a little girl. "I think I'm falling for you," she said.

I closed my eyes and gritted my teeth. "I feel the same way."

"Promise you'll never hurt me."

I pulled her closer. "You have nothing to worry about."

The next few days and weeks, I did very well with my vow. The day after Amber and I slept together, I called MaryAnn and said that I needed time to think about things and to not call for a while. I was convinced that within a few weeks she would find someone anyway.

Chapter 6

My relationship with Amber was getting better and better. She was everything MaryAnn wasn't. With MaryAnn, any conversation regardless of subject would be turned around so that we'd end up talking about her. Amber really listened to what I had to say.

MaryAnn would drive me nuts every time we went out. She would always be looking at other guys; kind of flirting with her eyes. She claimed that it was because she liked to watch people, but I found it strange that the people she watched were primarily good-looking men. Amber only had eyes for me. There were a lot of times I'd catch her staring; in the coffeehouse, at the mall, in restaurants. People around us never distracted her.

The only problem was that I'd find myself thinking that she was nowhere near as pretty as MaryAnn. MaryAnn was a head-turner. She'd walk into a room and automatically be the person everyone wanted to see. Amber's beauty was much more subtle. She had beautiful eyes, and a much better body than anyone would think by just looking at her, but people wouldn't stop what they were doing when she walked by like they did with MaryAnn. It's probably superficial to focus on physical attraction, but there's something very gratifying when most men wish they were you. I missed that.

A few weeks after we started officially dating, Amber introduced me to her mom and step-dad. They were nice people, but a bit overwhelming. All her step-dad wanted to talk about was how the decay of western society centered on the fact that parents couldn't discipline their kids. I agreed with him to a point, but the guy was militant.

They took an immediate liking to me, and said over and over again that I was such a gentleman. If only they knew. Amber did have an older step-sister, and I made it a point to let Rob know. The sister was no raving beauty, but beggars can't be choosers. Unfortunately –or maybe fortunately-- that fizzled about an hour into their first date.

The first time I was over there we had a simple dinner. The food was really good, and I complimented her mother on the meal which went a long way toward making a good impression. We left and walked out to the car. I opened her door so she could get in and heard applause coming from her house. I looked up to see the whole family watching us from the porch.

That night when we got to her place, there was a baseball game on television, and she didn't complain a bit when I sat down to watch. I don't know why, but everything that happened in our relationship I compared to my experience with MaryAnn; like it was some sort of game where one was pitted against the other. We sat there, watching the game when Amber looked up at me.

"I've been thinking," she said, sounding tentative. "How would you feel about moving in with me?"

We had only been dating for maybe month, and I worried maybe that would be rushing things. I knew I should say something to that effect, but chickened out.

"Sure, sounds great," I said. My life would be immensely improved if I'd grow a spine.

"I know you're sleeping on the couch there, and you spend the weekends with me anyway…"

"I think it's a great idea."

I was digging an even deeper hole. "If you want, you can start moving your boxes over this weekend," she offered.

I knew my brother would be thrilled. Other than the obvious benefit of giving him a drinking buddy, all I did was get in the way. Maybe it was a good development. MaryAnn wouldn't have a way to contact me, and I could have a place where I wasn't sleeping in the living room. I was actually beginning to enjoy the cold showers every morning, but I could still take them if I wanted. Yes, this wasn't a bad development after all.

Once I got home I told my brother the news. "Hey, that works out perfectly," he said.

"What's that supposed to mean?"

"I'm thinking about getting a dog."

I looked over. "A dog? But you hate dogs."

"Yeah, I know."

"In fact, hate isn't a strong enough word. After that little mutt next door bit you when we were kids, and then mysteriously disappeared, you said the only thing that would have been better is if it happened to every dog on the planet."

"I know all that."

"So why would you get a dog?" I asked. "That doesn't make any sense."

"Have you seen that girl in the park? The blonde chick?"

"You gotta be kidding me. The dog-walker girl? You want to get a dog to meet the dog-walker girl?"

"What kind of dog do you think I should get?"

"You're serious about this?" I asked. "You're getting a dog to meet a girl?"

"So?"

"This is a new low even for you."

"You think it's a bad idea?"

"Come on, Rob. Think about it for a second. What's the endgame here? You get a dog you don't want to meet a girl you don't know. Seriously, what's the chances she's single? And if she's single, what's the chance she'll go out with you?"

He was looking at the ceiling with a contemplative expression. "I definitely don't want a big dog, but I don't want something small either."

"Ask yourself this. How long each day is she going to walk it, an hour? What are you going to do with the other twenty-three hours? Who's going to take care of it when you're at work?"

"She will," he said defensively.

"Why don't you just ask the girl out? She'll shoot you down, and you'll save a couple hundred bucks."

"But I already told her I had a dog," he said. He took a piece of paper out of his pocket. "She gave me her number."

I looked at him for a long moment. "Thank you," I said.

His eyebrows wrinkled. "What's that supposed to mean?"

"This whole thing with MaryAnn and Amber has made me feel like a complete and utter asshole. But you? Asking a girl to walk a dog you don't even own just to get her number? I tell you, brother, I'm feeling a lot better."

"So you think telling a little white lie to get a girl's number is worse than sleeping with two women at the same time?"

I looked at him and we both started to laugh. "You're right," I said as I walked to the fridge and grabbed two beers. "No, you're absolutely right. I'm an asshole and you're pathetic."

I handed him a beer, and we touched them together. We sat there drinking them, and a few minutes later he asked, "So what kind of dog do you think I should get?"

I was definitely going to miss my brother.

Chapter 7

It was a Wednesday when Amber invited me to live with her, and the next day MaryAnn called out of the blue.

"Hey, cheese head," she said when I came on the line.

That was a new one. "How are things going?" I asked.

"Really good. I met this guy named Louie and we have a lot in common. It's like we're the same person."

Hearing that hurt a lot more than I expected. "I'm glad you're happy."

"I just wanted to give you a call and see how you were doing. I thought maybe you missed me."

"Yeah, I'm doing great. I'm kind of seeing this girl, Amber. She's really sweet."

"Is she as pretty as me?"

"She's very pretty."

"I didn't think so," she said.

I rolled my eyes. "Whatever. I hope things work out between you and Guido."

"Louie," she corrected. "It's a hell of a lot better than Houston."

It felt good to press her buttons. "It doesn't matter what his name is. I hope he makes you happy. Send him my regards."

"You're an asshole," she said before hanging up the phone.

I sat down on the couch, feeling depressed. I had told myself that I wanted her to find someone else, but I didn't know how to feel now that she had. I knew she didn't belong to me, but I thought of her as mine. Even after she cheated, she always came back. She chose me. Now she was choosing someone else.

Part of me wondered if we could have made it work if I had taken her back. Regardless of how much better Amber treated me, MaryAnn was the one I loved. The thought disturbed me. Did I still love MaryAnn?

I got up and slowly got my boxes together, mulling things over in my mind. I stacked all my stuff against the wall, figuring to take it out to the car the next morning.

At work, I found out that Amber and I would no longer be seated together. Amber had been disappointed, but I figured it would be better for our relationship. There was something oppressive about being with a person twenty-four hours a day.

I woke up Friday morning, relieved that I wouldn't have to sleep on a foldout bed anymore. I put the boxes in my trunk and drove to work.

I was a lot more disappointed when they announced the new seating arrangement. The person I ended up sitting next to was Dave Wesselman, Amber's old boyfriend.

We were seated at our desks when the announcement was made, and Amber turned around. "They put me next to Jay Theissen," she complained. "Every time he talks to me he stares at my tits."

"I got you beat," I said.

She looked at my screen and immediately brought a hand to her mouth. "Should be interesting," I said. "I'm sure he knows by now."

"God. And he asked me when I broke up with him if it was to go out with you."

"That'll make it even more interesting when you come over to talk."

She gave me a horrified look. "There's no way."

"And you know he'll always be looking over my shoulder trying to read the emails you send."

"He's gotta be over it by now."

I smiled. "I don't know, darlin.' You'd be pretty hard to forget."

She rolled her eyes. "Seriously, I won't be able to come to your desk again. I doubt he'd say anything, but still…"

"What about me?" I asked. "You know if go over there, Jay will stare at my tits."

She laughed. "I'll miss you, though. We'll still be able to go for walks, right?"

I pretended to consider it. "I don't know," I said slowly. "Dave might need a shoulder to cry on."

"That stopped being funny five minutes ago."

Not long after that, Dave stopped by and stuck out his hand. "Looks like we're going to be neighbors," he said.

I selected a spot on his forehead because I knew I'd crack if I looked him in the eye. "Looking forward to it," I said, taking his hand.

"Hi, Amber. You're looking good."

He gave her an appraising look, and I think she might have blushed. "Thank you," she said.

He stood there for a few more awkward moments, then waved and walked away.

"See. No problem at all," I said, after he left.

The rest of the workday was chaotic, but we were still able to walk out the door at exactly 5:00. I followed her to the apartment, and we unloaded the boxes in a matter of minutes. Unpacking everything took significantly longer. Luckily her old roommate had left a dresser so I was able to stow most of my clothes.

I had a lot of pictures, mostly of my family and MaryAnn, and Amber insisted on going through them all. That took the better part of an hour. She made lots of comments on how pretty MaryAnn was, and every time would look over for my reaction, like I was supposed to say, "Not as pretty as you, dear," or "She's not that pretty in person." Instead, I just nodded.

I have three more brothers and sisters not counting Rob, and she tried very hard to remember all of their names.

It was a little weird when we went to bed, which didn't make sense. I'd spent the last two weekends there, but this was different. It took me quite a while to drift off to sleep. The rest of the weekend was fairly routine.

Monday, though, was anything but. The first hour of the workday was spent moving my stuff from my old desk to the new one, and putting everything in place. Dave and I made small talk about the upcoming NFL season, baseball; stuff like that for the first hour or so.

Right in the middle of our conversation, he asked, "Are you dating Amber?" Very casual about it, like he was asking for a pencil. I looked at him for a few seconds, realized my mouth was open, closed it, and pretended to move things around on my desk.

"What do you mean?"

"Are you dating her? Going out? Seeing each other outside of work?" Like I was some idiot. I turned around and looked at him.

"Why are you asking me that?" I asked, trying to smile.

"A couple months ago I asked if you had a girlfriend and you said you were engaged."

He still wasn't acting confrontational; more like we were having a discussion. "At the time I was."

"But now you're dating Amber."

I hesitated. "Yeah."

"Do you love her?"

"Wait a second," I said, putting up a hand. "Where is this coming from?"

"Because I loved her."

"Look, man... Dave," I said, trying my best not to sound condescending. "I think it's great you love her, loved her, whatever. She's a great girl. But this is a conversation I'd rather not have here at work."

He nodded. "Okay, you're right. No big deal."

The rest of the day, he acted like the conversation never took place. I don't think I turned around once for fear that it would spark another outburst. Let me tell you: staring at nothing but a computer screen, never looking anywhere else, makes for a very long day. I actually did a lot of work. The way I saw it, I was going to have a very productive couple of months.

I considered telling Amber about what had happened with Dave, but decided not to. Hopefully the issue was dead and gone.

Tuesday, however, proved that wasn't the case. I was sitting at my desk when Dave tapped me on the shoulder.

"I wanted to apologize for yesterday," he said. "I know I acted like a complete ass."

I shrugged. "Don't worry about it."

"The thing is, I talked to Amber after we broke up a couple times, but then she refused to talk to me anymore."

I nodded and turned back to my computer, hoping he'd let it drop. No such luck.

"I know you said you didn't want to talk about it here at work, and I completely understand." Now he was whispering. "I thought maybe we could talk about it after work. We could have dinner, or something. My treat."

"We'll see."

"I just didn't get any closure."

The poor guy must have thought I was Dr. Phil. "I'll talk to Amber about it," I said.

He wasn't a bad looking guy, and it wasn't like Amber was the prettiest girl in the world. It didn't make any sense why he couldn't let her go. Worst-case scenario he could try the Internet. That had to be better than asking his ex-girlfriend's new boyfriend to break bread.

That evening I told Amber about our conversation. Naturally, she was mortified.

"He wanted to take you out to dinner?" she asked.

I nodded. "The guy was practically in tears."

"Do you want me to talk to him? He tried calling me a few times afterwards, but there was nothing left to say."

"He said he wasn't able to get closure." I used the first two fingers on each hand to indicate quotes on the word closure.

"He said that? Closure?"

I nodded. "Like I'm his therapist."

"So do you want me to talk to him? What if he wants to go out?"

"If you don't, my life at work is going to be hell until the next shift switch."

She got up and started pacing. "God, it's been over three months. You'd think he'd have let it go already."

"I guess you're a hard habit to break," I said. Then I started singing the lyrics to the song.

"Why does everything have to be movie lines and song lyrics with you?"

I picked her up, and she squealed as I put her over my shoulder and carried her back to the bedroom. I had my way with her, and then she had her way with me. At some point I fell asleep. When I woke up, she was looking over, staring at me with a small smile.

"You make such cute sounds when you sleep," she said. I rolled over and covered the back of my head with a pillow.

"Why can't any man take a compliment?" she asked.

"I don't think that qualifies as a compliment."

I was almost back to sleep when she asked, "So what do you think?"

I raised my head. "Think about what?"

"Dave. Do you think I should see him or not?"

I put my head back on my pillow. "It would make things a lot easier on me, that's for sure."

"He said closure?"

I raised my eyebrows, and that ended the conversation. The rest of the week, I didn't so much as glance at Dave, at least not on purpose. It felt like my eyes were going to fall out of my head, staring at the screen all day.

On Friday, my boss called me into her office. She was an attractive older woman with dark hair that was turning gray. She was built like a fire hydrant; short and about the same shape all the way down. Most of the times I met with her she'd say I wasn't working up to my potential, or something similar.

"I wanted to tell you how pleased I am with your work during the past week," she said. "It looks like you've finally taken our conversations to heart."

I tried not to roll my eyes. "Doing my best, boss."

"Well I wanted you to know that I noticed, and I hope you keep up the good work." She drove the point home like she always did; pumping her fist a few times like she was celebrating.

"I appreciate that," I said, standing to leave.

"I hope you're not too distracted."

I stopped. "Distracted by what?"

She gave me an ambiguous smile. "She's quite a gal."

I laughed and walked back to my desk. I've always wondered why managers, especially women of that age, felt compelled to let you know that they see everything that's going on; like they don't miss a trick.

Plus the word "gal." Donna, my manager, used it at every opportunity. Sometimes I wanted to tell her to take that word back to the fifties and leave it where it belonged.

Other than those minor details, she wasn't bad to work for, a lot better than most of the other managers there, that's for sure.

Right before I left for the day, I told Dave that Amber would call him over the weekend to have a talk. He asked if I would go, too, and seemed shocked when I said "no." Amber called him and arranged to meet on Saturday at noon.

Once she left Saturday morning, I got dressed and drove downtown. I parked on Third Street and went to the bookstore in the Tower Place mall. The place was streaming with people and after looking around for a minute or so I walked to the Starbucks that was less than a block away. My plan was to drink a frapuccino and read the paper for about a half hour, and then drive home.

Around the same time I got the sports section out of the paper bin, MaryAnn came through the revolving door. Our eyes locked almost immediately and she waved. Not sure how to respond, I waved back and walked over to where I had left my drink. She joined me not long after.

"I figured I'd run into you here sooner or later," she said.

I shrugged. "I don't really come down her very much anymore."

"Are you kidding me?" she asked, slapping me on the arm like we were college buddies. "You practically lived here when we met."

"Things change."

Her eyes turned to slits, but I pretended not to notice and sipped my drink. "Are you still seeing the same girl?" she asked.

I nodded. "What about you? Are you still seeing Guido or whatever his name is?"

She gave me her pissed-off look. "He's not Italian. His name is Louie, which is French. And yes, I'm still seeing him."

"Things going good?"

She gave a half-hearted shrug. "It's okay. I miss you, though."

I tried to act cool, but knew I couldn't pull it off for long. "Is he here with you?"

"No, he had to work."

"Oh, yeah?" I asked. "What's he do?"

She looked down. "He works at the Quikstop in Covington."

"I guess someone has to do it," I said, trying not to chuckle. "What about your girlfriend? Where is she today?"

"She's seeing an old boyfriend. They had some stuff to work out." She laughed. "Isn't that ironic?"

We both sipped our drinks, looking back and forth for a few minutes. "Have you eaten?" I asked, surprised when the words came out of my mouth.

She shook her head. "You got somewhere in mind?"

"I'm sure Rock Bottom is open," I said, automatically knowing it was a mistake. That was where we'd had our first date, and nostalgia was the last thing I needed. I think the same thought was going through her mind.

It was a warm, windy day and paper was blowing everywhere. It was almost impossible walking into the wind without putting your head down. MaryAnn reached out and grabbed my hand, and shamefully I let her do it. We walked like that across Fountain Square and into the restaurant.

We chitchatted back and forth about nothing in particular, and I tried to steer the conversation away from Amber as much as possible. After our food was served, the talk ended for the most part; just a stray word here and there. As I sat looking across the table I wondered how I could have ever thought I was over her. I wanted to reach over and run my fingers through that kinky, blond hair.

I ordered a Cincinnati American Light after the meal, and MaryAnn did the same. Amber would be getting home soon, but I pushed the thought from my mind. I dragged out lunch as long as I could until we both agreed that it was time to go.

I walked her back to her car and opened the driver side door, expecting that to be the end of it. She stood on tiptoe to kiss me, and I pulled her close. Next thing I knew we were necking in the street like a couple of teenagers. She looked at me with such a hunger, and I'm sure I did the same. After another furious round of kissing I pushed her in the car and then climbed over her into the passenger seat. She didn't start her car; just looked at me like she was waiting for me to tell her what to do. I thought about it for a second, then opened the door and got out. I didn't look back, knowing full well where we'd end up if I did. Once I got behind the wheel of my car, I breathed a sigh of relief. The temptation had been resisted.

Chapter 8

I drove home and sure enough, Amber's car was in the parking lot. I checked my face in the rearview mirror to make sure there was no lipstick and walked in.

"How did it go?" I asked.

She rolled her eyes. "Don't ask. He cried like a baby from the moment we sat down. He kept saying he loved me and that no other guy could ever treat me as good as he did."

"What did you tell him?"

"I told him to consider therapy, but there was no way we'd ever get back together."

I laughed. "You said that? Get therapy?"

She smiled and shrugged. "What did he say?" I asked.

"He kept saying he loved me."

"Do you think it ever sunk in that it was over?"

"God, I hope so. I don't think I could go through that again."

"Maybe it's a good thing, though. Did I tell you what Donna said Friday?"

She shook her head. "She said that my work has gotten a lot better over the last week or so," I said.

"You're such a dork."

"So you don't think you two have a future?"

"I'm a one-man woman," she said, coming over and burying her face against my chest. She held me for a few more seconds and then sniffed my shirt a couple times. "What's that smell?"

I lifted the bottom of the shirt to my nose. "I don't know. Fabric Softener?"

"No, it's woman's perfume," she said, her forehead wrinkling.

Oh, crap. "I haven't worn this shirt in a while, but I can't imagine why it smells that way." I lifted it up and smelled it again. "I don't smell anything."

She held my eyes for a few beats, and I did my best not to blink. "I don't like that perfume," she said finally. "Make sure to wash that shirt."

I immediately took it off and threw it in the laundry basket.

I was nervous on Monday because of Amber's little meeting with Dave. I got there about ten minutes before my shift was scheduled to start and stayed in the cafeteria until the last possible moment. He was at his desk when I got there, and I walked past like he was a plant.

I stared at my computer doing what I was paid to do, trying my best to make the boss proud. A couple hours into the day, I heard Dave say my name. I ignored him, hoping he'd take the hint, but he said it again, this time a little louder. I turned in my swivel chair to face him, eyes upraised.

"I wanted to thank you for letting me meet with Amber," he said.

"No problem," I said, turning around. Apparently he didn't take the hint because he continued. "I'm also sorry I said some of the things I did last week."

"No apology necessary," I said, pretending to work.

Finally, he figured it out. I thought that would be the end of our conversations for a while, but about half an hour later he started again.

"Me and a couple buddies are getting a team together for a league at Sports of All Sorts, and I was thinking maybe you could play with us."

No way in hell. Instead I said, "Oh, yeah? What day of the week will you guys be playing?"

"Sunday nights."

I gave him a pained expression. "I always spend Sunday nights with my mom. Maybe next time."

What was it about using my mom as an excuse? I definitely needed better material.

"Let me know if you change your mind."

I didn't even respond. When I got home, I had a message from my brother asking me to give him a call. My brother hates talking on the phone, so usually when he calls it's because someone is sick or dead.

"What's wrong?" I asked when he picked up.

"MaryAnn called and asked you to call her back," he said, sounding defensive.

"You scared me to death. I thought there was some kind of accident."

"Whatever. I didn't figure you'd want me leaving a message like that on your machine. Maybe next time I'll just give her your number."

I rolled my eyes. "You're such a drama queen. It's not me who hates to talk on the phone. When was the last time you called me?"

There were a few beats of silence. "So you coming over to watch the Reds game tonight?"

"You miss me?" I asked.

"You're an idiot."

"Because it sounds like you miss me."

"If you come, pick up a twelve pack and a couple bags of pretzels."

With that, he hung up. Amber was sitting next to me, so calling back MaryAnn wasn't an option.

"What did he want?" she asked. She tried to act casual about it, but the urgency in her voice gave her away. The first thing that went through my mind was to lie, but I thought better of it.

"My ex-girlfriend asked me to call."

She looked at me for a long moment. "What do you think it's about?"

Now was the time to lie. "She probably found some of my stuff," I said, turning on the television. I needed an excuse to look somewhere else.

"Are you going to call her back?"

"You mean now?"

She nodded. It was my turn to act casual. I propped one leg up on the coffee table, and slung an arm over the couch. "Do you think I should?" I asked.

She nodded again. "It's probably not a good idea," I said.

"Why?" she asked, a little bite to her voice. "Are you ashamed of me?"

I put down the remote. "More like I don't want her to have this number."

"Are you going to call her later?"

I sighed and leaned my head back. "I don't know, Amber," I said, acting more pissed off than I really was. "I'll probably have to at some point so I can find out what she wants."

We sat there watching television for about fifteen minutes, neither of us saying anything.

"My brother asked me to come over and watch the game tonight," I said. "You want to go?"

"It's up to you."

"Nothing better to do," I said, scratching my nose.

She walked back to the bedroom and didn't come out for about twenty minutes. A couple times I almost went back to see if everything was okay, but I knew if I did she would bring up the whole thing with MaryAnn. I should have followed my instincts and lied about it, told her something about my mom needing to talk to me.

We drove over to my brother's place and she didn't say anything until we got into the parking lot. "Do you still love her?" she asked in a small voice.

I gripped the steering wheel as hard as I could with both hands. "Yes and no."

She gave me a look like I was supposed to continue. "She was my first real girlfriend, and obviously the first girl, the only girl, I've ever asked to marry me. Those feelings don't go away overnight.

"But she also cheated on me twice, and there's no going back from that. Once someone cheats there's no point. I could never trust her again. Even if I wasn't living with you, even if I had to live in a cardboard box; no matter what, I wouldn't go back to her."

Hearing myself say it, I knew it was true. She smiled, happy with the explanation. "Why didn't you say that in the first place?"

She was in much better spirits when we walked into Rob's apartment. Of course, he was sprawled out on the couch, four empty beer cans in front of him. He'd gotten an English bulldog and it attacked me the moment I walked through the door. After a minute or so of sniffing my crotch, it finally left me alone. Rob looked up, and then down at my hands.

"Where's the booze?" he asked.

"I knew I forgot something. I'll be right back," I said, then looked over at Amber. "You want to come along or just stay here?"

"I'll go," she said.

"Why don't you stay?" my brother asked. "Give us a chance to catch up."

The sly look on his face worried me. "I'll just stay then," Amber said.

"Be back in five minutes."

It actually took closer to thirty. I don't know why, but every Friday there are about twenty people in line at the local supermarket, but only two cashiers.

I got back to the apartment with the twelve-pack and walked in to see my brother and Amber in the middle of what seemed to be a serious conversation. Rob looked up when I came through the door, then back down at my hands.

"Where's the pretzels?" he asked.

"If you want them that bad, you can drive to the supermarket."

He complained a little as I put the twelve-pack in the refrigerator.

"Hey, sensuous," he said, pointing at his can. Without saying anything I grabbed three cans and sat between my brother and Amber, handing each a beer.

Amber looked back and forth between us. "Why did you call him sensuous?" she asked.

"My brother thinks he's Bill Murray," I said.

"It's actually saying, 'sensuous up, grab me another beer,'" he said, sounding pleased with himself.

"And that's a line only Bill Murray could make work," I said.

"I think it's cute," she said.

"Thank you," said my brother, looking even more pleased.

"Baby's are cute, puppies are cute. That's just stupid."

"He's still got big brother envy," Rob said. "Very, very sad."

"Speaking of sad, how's it going with the dog-walker girl?" I asked.

"I'm still waiting for the right time to make my move," he said defensively.

"Three months and you still haven't found the stones to ask her out?"

He glared at me. "We're still in the 'feeling each other out' phase."

"You wait too long, she's going to think you're gay," I said, taking a long swallow from my beer.

"She knows I'm not gay. I told her I had a girlfriend, but we just broke up."

"First you lie about having a dog, and now you're making up a girlfriend? Next thing, you'll own a pet unicorn and an invisible rocket ship. Have you even named the dog yet?"

He hesitated. "Herbert."

I looked at Amber and then back at him. "You named the dog Herbert?"

"I had to come up with something."

"But Herbert?"

"It's better than Houston."

"You heard that, Amber," I said. "Back me up when I tell Dad what he said."

We went back and forth like that most of the night. I stopped drinking at the end of the fifth inning so I'd be sober enough to drive. The Reds were down by six runs in the seventh inning, so I told Amber it was time to go. Right as we were getting up to leave, the phone rang.

"Just a second," my brother said once he answered the phone. He held it out, a guilty expression on his face. There was no doubt in my mind who it was. I took the phone and started to walk back to the bathroom. One look at Amber told me that if I did, I'd never hear the end of it so I sat down beside her.

"I was hoping you could do me a huge favor," she said, after we'd gone through the introductions.

"Okay," I said, more as a question.

"Do you think you could pick up an accident report for me? It's downtown at the courthouse on Eighth Street."

"You can't do it?"

"I'm taking classes this summer, and I can't get there while they're open. If you do this for me, I'll owe you for life."

"Okay, fine," I said. How stupid was I?

"Do you want to come over?"

Actually," I said, looking over at Amber with a smile. "I'm sitting here with my girlfriend and my brother watching baseball."

"Did you tell her what happened earlier today?"

"Yeah, we're having a good time."

"I'll take that as a 'no.'"

"Exactly," I said, giving Amber another smile.

"Is she as good in bed as me?"

"Tell her I said hi," Amber whispered.

"Yeah," I said. "Amber says to tell you hi."

"Do you think of me when you're having sex with her?"

"Okay, well I have to go. Take care," I said, disconnecting the line.

I stretched my arms above my head in an exaggerated yawn. "Well, it's been fun, bro, but we're going to take off."

"Can't you stay until the end?"

"You ready, sweetie?" I asked, ignoring him.

We got in the car, and she squeezed my knee. "What did she need?"

I already had my lie prepared. "She said she had my passport and would drop it off at my mom's." Apparently, that satisfied her.

We were in bed that night, and the MaryAnn's words kept going through my mind. It was her face I was seeing every time I closed my eyes. Try as I might, I couldn't get the picture out of my head. I even found myself wishing that Amber would turn into MaryAnn. Amber gave me everything I could ever want in a girlfriend, but I could never look at her the same way I did MaryAnn.

It was a real enigma. One way or the other, I'd be settling. Lying in bed that night, I wondered if the honorable thing to do was break up with Amber so that she could find a man who could give her the things she deserved. The only reason I could come up with to stay together was completely selfish: I didn't want to be alone. Once again, I couldn't get away from the idea that I was a horrible person. For whatever reason, it made me smile. What a bastard!

That next Monday during my lunch break I picked up MaryAnn's accident report. I called her at school from a payphone downtown to let her know that I'd drop it off within the next couple of days.

I looked for an opportunity, and on Wednesday when Amber said that her family invited us to dinner, I feigned being sick. I waited until she was gone for half an hour, and then drove over to see MaryAnn. I fully expected to hand her the accident report and go home, but when she asked me to sit down and have a drink, I did.

One drink led to another and before I knew it, she was dragging me back to the bedroom. After it was over, she kept saying that there was no way I could resist her; basically saying that she had some kind of voodoo power over me. I asked her what she would say to Louie, and she said as long as he didn't find out what difference would it make. I figured the same was true for Amber. MaryAnn tried to talk me into staying, but I managed to get away.

I was in the shower when I heard Amber come through the door. Let me tell you, I soaped down and scrubbed my body like it's never been scrubbed before; so hard, in fact, I could feel raw areas when I toweled off. After I came out of the shower, she asked if I was feeling better and I said I did. She never suspected a thing.

The next few weeks, I treated her like a queen; even better than I'd ever treated MaryAnn. I sent her flowers, and complimented her on everything. I even suggested we spend more time with her family. I didn't say "no" to a single thing she asked.

The times I felt the guiltiest was when we were at her folk's house. They couldn't have been nicer. We'd play cards, eat together, interact; they welcomed me like family. A couple times, we went bowling. I'd always hated doing things like that in the past, but they made it fun. And Amber was incredibly sexy when she bowled.

I knew if her family knew the truth about my indiscretions, they would have me stoned; maybe even worse, and if Amber found out, she would never speak to me again.

During that time I swore never to see MaryAnn again. The trouble was that she was always on my mind.

After a while of going through that range of emotions, I talked myself into believing that if I saw her again, told her about how much crap she'd put me through, and what a complete bitch she was, maybe then I could put her behind me.

Another week or so went by before I emailed MaryAnn and asked if she wanted to get together. A few days later she emailed me back, said that things were getting serious between her and Louie, and it wouldn't be a good idea. Reading that was like taking an arrow to the heart; unbelievable pain.

Things began to improve between Amber and me after that, and I started to think about things long-term. Maybe waiting another year or so to propose, saving up money to buy a ring, even trying to get a house together. I really thought things were going well. Boy was I wrong.

We were at my mom's house for dinner, and I was out talking to my brothers and sisters on the porch when Amber walked up to me. It was obvious she was unhappy.

"I need to talk to you," she snapped.

I exchanged nervous looks with my siblings, and followed her outside. We walked to the edge of my parent's property, and she turned. If her face had been any more red, she'd have burst into flame.

"I just talked to your mother," she said.

"Okay?"

"She's never had the flu in her life."

I raised an eyebrow. "What's your point?"

"You remember our first night together? The first time we made love?"

Right then I remembered. She continued. "You said you couldn't come over right away because your mother had the flu."

I wished I'd brought something to eat or drink when she asked me to follow her. It would give me an opportunity to buy a little time. Unfortunately, I wasn't that farsighted.

"I was scared," I mumbled.

She snorted, and kept staring at me. I knew I had to tell the truth. "All right, okay," I said, looking off into the distance. "MaryAnn called saying we needed to work something out and I went over there."

"What exactly did you need to discuss?"

"I don't remember," I said, feeling the heat coming up my neck and spreading over my face.

"Did you sleep with her?"

"No," I said, trying to act like that was the most ridiculous question I'd ever heard. "God, no."

"Have you ever lied to me about anything else?"

I was in a real pickle. "I didn't want to lie to you then, but I was afraid you'd blow it out of proportion.

She stared at me for a little longer, the challenge still in her eyes. "If you ever lie about anything again; anything, and that's it."

"I'll never lie to you again," I lied. "I swear."

Her eyes started to well up as she put her arms around me and pressed her head into my chest. "God, Amber," I said. "I love you."

It was the first time I'd told her that, and I could tell it meant a lot. "I love you, too," she said as I leaned down to kiss her. Talk about guilt.

Chapter 9

After the confrontation I felt even worse which is saying something because I was already feeling pretty bad. Once again, I vowed to never mess around again. Unlike the other vows, this one I swore to keep.

Amber's birthday was July 28, and even though I thought it was a big mistake she insisted we invite both of our families. Talk about a study in contrasts. In TV terms, her family was "The Andy Griffith Show," and mine was "Married with Children." Her family was one big supportive unit. No one had a bad word to say. Everyone in my family cared about each other, and if there was trouble everyone would be there, but when we got together, it was a nonstop roast.

We agreed to have the party at her parent's place. My sister and brother-in-law were the first of my family members to arrive, and they set the tone for the evening. They came through the door arguing about my brother-in-law's ability to drive, or lack thereof. My sister is a hellcat, and once she gets started, Katie-bar-the-door.

I could tell that Amber's family was horrified, but that was just the beginning. My brother, Rob, walked in a few minutes later. With no formal introduction, he walked over to the refrigerator like he owned the place. He opened it, looked around for a while, and then asked if they had any American beer; how the foreign beers weren't easily digested.

My parents arrived not long after, and my mom was dressed in her traditional sweat pants that were about three inches too short, droopy white socks, and a thin, bleached-out t-shirt. My dad had on cut-off jean shorts, short-sleeve button-down shirt, and raggedy tennis shoes with no socks. Obviously my parents aren't snappy dressers.

My brother, Austin, and his wife came in next, both wearing their "I'm with Stupid" t-shirts that they loved so much. Thankfully, they were my only siblings who were able to make it.

gly enough, everyone got along throughout dinner, and I I had worried needlessly. That changed after Amber's mom started clearing the dishes. To give a little background, my dad is a dyed-in-the-wool republican. He spent twenty years in the Army, and as far as he's concerned democrats are the spawn of hell. Amber's family is the exact opposite. Her stepfather is the union leader at the plant where he works, and her mother volunteers for a lot of local campaigns. I knew we were doomed when the subject of politics came into the conversation.

My brother was the one who stirred the pot when he started talking about the stimulus package. I had made the mistake of telling him about her family's views.

"That's what we get for electing a community organizer," my dad said.

Amber's dad sat up in his chair. "I think President Obama has done a great job with the mess he inherited."

Dad snickered. "Are you kidding? Five years ago this idiot was arranging bake sales and now he's running the greatest country in the world. It's no wonder our economy is in such bad shape. By the time this jackass is out of office we'll all be speaking Chinese."

Her step-dad looked uncomfortable. "I think he's very qualified to get us through this."

"The man doesn't know his ass from his elbow," my dad said, taking another swallow of his beer. "First he gives away a trillion dollars on corporate bailouts, and now he's talking about mandated healthcare? The douchebag obviously thinks he's entitled to take a giant dump on the Constitution. Our founding fathers are rolling over in their graves."

"I respect your opinion, but I've met the man. He's a standup guy, a leader."

My dad stared at him for a few seconds, and I was afraid he might do something crazy. "Well, it's your house so you believe whatever the hell you want."

My mom and Amber's mom were trading nervous glances, and it was obvious that neither wanted the conversation to continue. "Who wants dessert?" her mom asked.

I could tell that my dad had more to say on the subject, but to his credit he kept his mouth shut. We all went into the living room, and Amber's mom came out of the kitchen carrying a large sheet cake with white frosting. The cake had big flowers on it, and an inscription that read "Happy Birthday, Poodle" in bold, blue letters. Her mother was in the process of putting on the candles, when Rob looked over with a smirk.

"Poodle? Where the hell did that come from?" he asked. My brother isn't known for having tact.

Amber's face got a little red. "My middle name is Sue, and somehow that evolved into poodle."

"I think it's cute," I said, glaring at him.

"Maybe if you like being named after a dog," he muttered, and I could see Amber's mother making a point to look away. I vowed to get revenge if he ever got a girlfriend. I wasn't holding my breath.

After we sang happy birthday and Amber blew out the candles, my brother helped himself to the first piece of cake. The rest of my family wasn't far behind. I've always said that my family could never embarrass me, but at that moment I was teetering on the edge.

Amber's family politely sat in their seats waiting for mine to finish. We all took our plates out on the deck and watched the sun go down. Even my dad complimented the view. One by one, my siblings and their spouses left, leaving only my parents. We sat and talked for a few minutes -- obviously not about politics -- and my dad said they had to go.

"You have a real nice place," my dad said, sticking out his hand. Amber's stepdad shook it, and put his hand on my dad's shoulder.

"It was nice meeting you, Mr. Thomas."

"You, too, even if you are a democrat." He laughed, acting like it was a joke, but I knew he wasn't kidding. Her step-dad tried to laugh, too, but it came out more as a "huh" than a "ha."

After they were gone, Amber's step-dad turned to me.

"I like your family," he said.

"Well, that's nice of you to say."

"I'm serious," he said, bunches his eyebrows together in a contemplative frown. "They have character."

"Well, you never have to wonder what they're thinking," her mother chimed in.

Amber and I left not long after, and I felt fairly confident that would be the last time she asked to bring our families together. After that fiasco, if we ever got married we'd have to elope.

By the end of August I'd practically forgotten about MaryAnn. I was happy with Amber; happier than I'd been my entire life. I hadn't seen MaryAnn since our chance encounter downtown, and I hadn't once called to hear her voice.

Labor Day was a great day. My family has a huge fireworks spectacular every year, and we sat out under the stars curled up together watching the swirling colors and listening to the explosions. At that moment, I believed she and I would be together forever.

Amber loved everything about me; didn't try to change me. Even things about myself I didn't like: my ears that are slightly too big, and my hairline which is slowly receding, she didn't mind. To hear her tell it, those flaws made me more endearing.

The euphoria was short-lived. The day after Labor Day, I took a vacation day in order to help my parents with the cleanup from the night before. Picking up all the litter and spent fireworks didn't take nearly as long as I expected, and by 11:00 we were done. I sat around talking to my parents for an hour or so, but around noon I started getting restless.

The weather was perfect; about seventy-five degrees and not a cloud in the sky. I drove to the Starbucks in downtown Cincinnati for a frapuccino, and planned to go from there to Sawyer Point next to the river where I would sit in the sun.

I had ordered my drink and was standing in line waiting for it to be made when I heard a familiar voice calling my name. I turned and found myself looking into the eyes of MaryAnn. Seeing her sitting there was a complete shock.

She smiled and expectantly patted the table in front of her. "How are you?" she asked as I continued to stare dumb-founded. I was utterly speechless. No response was coming to mind, so I turned to see if my drink was ready. I took my frapuccino off the counter and sat in the seat facing her. My conscience was telling me to get out of there as fast as possible, but my legs wouldn't cooperate.

"Wow!" I finally managed to say. "Definitely the last person I expected to see."

"I hope it's a good surprise."

I raised my eyebrows and shrugged non-committal. "I guess."

"Is that any way to talk to an old friend?" she asked. I didn't respond so she continued. "Are you still with the same girl?"

I nodded. "Sure am. What about you and whatever his name is?" I asked, even though I knew his name perfectly well.

"Louie," she sighed. "Unfortunately, Louie and I broke up. He just refused to treat me the way I deserve."

"That'll happen."

She appraised me after that statement, and I tried to look casual as I sipped my drink. "So what is that for you?" she asked. "You two have been together for what, four months? Five?"

I shrugged. "Something like that."

"Is it serious?"

"It's getting there."

"That's great, Houston. That's really great. I'm glad you're happy."

I mulled that over for a few seconds before I started feeling claustrophobic. "I better get going," I said, looking at the door.

"Do you want to go for a walk?"

"No, I have to get going. Places to go, people to see." Okay, fine, the line was corny, but it was the only thing that came to mind.

"I could walk you to your car," she offered.

I looked at the door again. "It's not far. Besides, you look comfortable."

I don't mind," she said, standing up.

I couldn't turn her down at that point. We stepped outside, me carrying my drink and her beside me. I had parked at a meter on Third Street, and probably had over an hour and a half before it expired. Hopefully, she wouldn't notice. It was only a block and a half, and we were there in a matter of minutes.

"It was good seeing you," I said, unlocking the door of my 2005 Corolla with the keyless remote.

She reached out and grabbed my hand, pulling us closer together. I made an attempt to get away, but it was half-hearted.

"Don't you have a kiss for an old friend?" she asked, giving me her sultry look.

My brain was telling me to say no, but the rest was saying something entirely different. I leaned down and kissed her. Our lips came together, and I realized what was missing in my relationship with Amber; the reason it felt incomplete.

"God, that feels good," she said, both hands right under my butt.

I started thinking about Amber. She gave me security, and I knew she'd love me forever. I also knew I'd never intentionally hurt her. And what about my vow, the one I'd sworn to keep?

"I can't do this," I said, pulling away.

She was all innocence. "Do what?"

"This. You. It," I said. "I can't do this to Amber."

"Amber has nothing to do with us."

I took a deep breath. I knew if I didn't walk away now, I'd get to the point where I couldn't. "No, but she has something to do with me. Goodbye, MaryAnn."

I was in my car and in the process of closing the door, when she stopped me. "Do you love her?" she asked.

I hesitated and then nodded. "Yeah, I think I do."

"As much as you loved me?"

I stared at my steering wheel. "I don't think I'll ever love someone that much again."

As soon as the words came out of my mouth, I knew I'd made a mistake. She bent down to kiss me and before long our hands were all over each other. Cars were honking, people were staring, but I didn't care. I knew I'd gotten to the point where I couldn't say "no."

"Come back with me," she said, hot breath on my neck. I didn't say anything, and she climbed into the passenger seat.

I can't say I didn't know what I was doing, because I did. I can't say that I was powerless to stop it, either, because it would be just as easy to say "no" as it was to say "yes." Her apartment was about a fifteen-minute drive away. The scenery went by in a blur, and everything seemed so familiar, like déjà vu. We got inside and went straight to the bedroom. The lovemaking was intense. Afterwards, lying next to her, smelling her hair, I wondered if maybe I'd done the right thing.

It wasn't until my drive home that I thought differently. I parked in the driveway, relieved that Amber hadn't gotten home yet. The neighborhood kids were playing basketball at the hoop on the far end of the parking lot, and one of the boys who I'd played a lot of ball with waved at me, but I ignored him.

I went through the door, took off my clothes and got in the shower. I dried off and was sitting in front of the television when Amber came through the door. She leaned down to give me a kiss, and I couldn't help but pull away. The only thing going through my mind was that she deserved better.

"Is everything okay?" she asked.

I nodded, but couldn't look up. "I was thinking maybe we could go out for dinner tonight."

"Okay," she said slowly. "Are you sure nothing's wrong?"

"I'm just a little tired."

She sat down beside me and started rubbing my leg. "If you're not feeling well we can stay here," she said, an invitation in her voice.

"I'm fine," I said, standing up and moving out of reach.

She gave me a peculiar frown and started back toward the bedroom. On her way past, she reached out, but I turned to avoid her touch.

Dinner was a difficult experience. She probably asked me twenty times if I was okay. The moment we got home, I went straight to bed without even bothering to take off my shoes.

"So this is what guilt feels like," I thought. I was treating Amber the same way that MaryAnn had treated me.

Amber walked in a few minutes later and asked me again what was wrong. I mumbled something about a headache. A few minutes later she came in again and removed my shoes. She got in bed next to me and put an arm over my hip. I thought about pushing it away, but I lacked the willpower.

At some point I drifted off to sleep, but woke up an hour or so later. Amber still had an arm around me, and was snoring softly. I turned slowly so I wouldn't wake her, and then stared at her for a long, long time. Before I knew it, I was crying like a baby. That lasted for a couple minutes, and she started to stir. I didn't want her to wake up and ask me if I was okay, so I got out of bed. The bed creaked a little and she looked up for a second, then quickly fell back to sleep.

I walked out and made myself a gin and orange juice, heavy on the gin, then sat on the couch. Staring at the ceiling, this time I decided not to make any vows.

"Amber and MaryAnn, MaryAnn and Amber," I muttered to myself. Style versus substance. I finished off my drink and mixed another one. I was about halfway through it when Amber came stumbling out of the bedroom. Feeling the buzz, seeing her, was enough to make me want to start crying again.

"What are you doing?" she asked.

I shrugged and she sat down next to me. "I don't deserve you," I said.

She smiled and rubbed my chest. "I don't know what you're talking about. I'm a lucky girl."

She loved saying that part about being a lucky girl. A little smile would come over her face, and she'd get a look in her eyes; a look that said I was the most important thing in her life.

"God, Amber," I said, closing my eyes. "You could do a lot better. A hell of a lot better."

"What are you talking about?" I glanced over and she had a wary expression, like she expected a confession would soon be forthcoming. I wasn't that drunk.

"No girl has ever treated me the way you do," I said. It was the truth.

"I'm a lucky girl," she whispered in my ear. She ran her hand down my stomach to the zipper of my jeans. I'd have probably pulled away if it hadn't been for the alcohol, but I let it happen. We rolled around on the living room floor, and I don't know why but I wanted to hurt her. I wanted to wrap my hands around her throat and squeeze.

Once it was over, I pretended to fall asleep there on the floor. My bladder was full and I really had to pee, but getting up would mean I'd have to talk to her. She kept shaking me, and I finally pretended to sleepwalk to the bathroom, and then to bed. Every hour or so during the night I got up to use the bathroom.

When seven o'clock came, I decided to call in sick. I pretended to be asleep until Amber left, and then went out to watch television. The only thing on was Sportscenter, and after watching it about four or five times, I picked up the phone and called MaryAnn. This time, there was no denial about my intentions.

"Hello," she said, sounding half-asleep.
"You want me to come over?"
She hesitated. "Give me a half hour?"

Chapter 10

The next month or so, I was over at MaryAnn's a lot; probably two or three times a week. I told Amber I was going to play basketball, shooting pool, whatever I could come up with. My brother, Rob was my co-conspirator. He said over and over again how he would kill for a girl like Amber; how she was a hell of a lot better than MaryAnn who he'd never cared for anyway. I knew where his loyalties lay, though, and I knew I could count on him. It made me happy that nothing had developed between him and Amber's sister.

MaryAnn started talking about a possible reunification. She didn't use the word, exactly, just hinted around how it would be nice to have me around more. I never considered it, though. The way I saw it, I had the best of both worlds.

The weeks became routine. A few passionate hours of reckless abandon, the rest of the time spent with practical security. Amber probably knew things weren't quite right because I remember thinking the same thing when I'd gone through it. I'm sure most people would say that being in the situation would make me feel guiltier about not being honest, but at the time I would have been happy to stay ignorant. I also know that what I had with MaryAnn was temporary. Amber was my future, but for now I wanted to live in the moment.

The best part was that I no longer felt guilty. I figured I could continue seeing them both indefinitely, but I came home from playing basketball one night in mid-October and found Amber crying on the couch. I put my gym bag on the floor and sat down beside her.

"What's wrong, poodle?" I asked. Since her birthday party, I'd been using the nickname.

She looked up. "Look at me. Don't look away."

I had a hunch what she was about to ask, and it made me happy that I'd really been playing basketball. I looked at her expectantly.

"Are you cheating on me?"

I avoided the impulse to blink. "What are you talking about?"

"Just answer the question."

"No," I said. "God, no. What would make you ask me that?"

"You told me yesterday that you went to play basketball." The day before I'd been with MaryAnn.

"Yeah?"

"After you left today, I called your brother and asked him if you'd gone bowling last night."

Uh oh. "Why would you do that?" I asked.

The phone rang, granting me a brief reprieve. "I'd better get that," I said walking toward the phone.

I held up an index finger. "Hello."

"Bro, are you alone?" Obviously, my brother Rob.

"No, how you doing?" I asked.

"If Amber asks what you were doing yesterday we went bowling."

"Well, why would you say you went bowling if it was you and Austin?"

He hesitated for a second. "What are you talking about?"

"Well, I'm sure you were drinking, but I told you I was going to play basketball. I never showed up at the bowling alley." I rolled my eyes at Amber, and shook my head.

"Oh, she's there, right?"

"Exactly. How did you guys do?"

"I guess I'm the designated asshole. You definitely owe me now. Two cases at least."

"I hope you weren't playing for money. Maybe if you didn't drink so much, you might win once in a while. And I hope you're happy." I tried to keep my tone casual and a smile on my face.

"So now part of this little dance is making me look like an alcoholic. That's cute."

"I think so, too."

"Uh huh, okay," he said.

"No. Don't worry about it. I'll talk to you later," I said, hanging up the phone.

"My brother called to apologize," I said.

Amber didn't look convinced. "There's more than just last night."

She started ticking off the reasons on her fingers. "A couple times you said you shot pool, but you didn't come home smelling like smoke. You don't ever want to have sex anymore. You're always so distant, like you want to be somewhere else. You don't even look at me the same."

She started crying again with the last statement, and I put both arms around her. I wasn't pulling it off like I had thought. "I'm sorry, poodle," I said, racking my brain for a plausible excuse. "I'm miserable at work…"

Not a very good one. Then it came to me. "And this whole relationship."

She broke away and looked up with the scared, tentative look women get when they think someone is about to break their heart.

"Maybe I'm crazy," I said kissing her. "After the whole thing with my ex-fiancé, I don't want to go through that again."

"So what are you saying? Do you want to slow things down?"

"No," I said, pulling her closer. "But I haven't felt this way about anybody, and we've only been going out for a couple months. I'm worried about getting hurt, that's all. I love you."

The look in her eyes said that the polar ice caps were melting. "I'm not going to hurt you," she said. "Why would I hurt the guy I want to spend the rest of my life with?"

She had a special ability to make me feel like a first-class asshole. "I'm sorry if I've done those things, or made you feel that way, or whatever," I said, stroking her hair. "I'll make it better. I promise."

"I'm worried about getting hurt, too," she said.

Here came that asshole feeling again. "I guess I'm just an amateur about this whole relationship thing. The only other girl I fell in love with broke my heart."

The make-up sex made me feel worse. I got up around two in the morning, went into the bathroom, and shut the door. One of the things I'd done since childhood was talk to my reflection when I'm trying to convince myself to do something. MaryAnn was my past. Amber was my future. The only way to move ahead was to stop looking back. There's a reason the windshield is bigger than the rearview mirror.

Remember that. Tell MaryAnn it was over. But I had told her it was over before. Probably seven or eight times, as a matter of fact.

Why did I keep going back? It sure wasn't her intelligence. She couldn't count to ten without using her fingers. It wasn't because she treated me well. She cheated on me at least twice. Maybe more. Probably more. The only thing she had over Amber was the way she looked, and how important was that anyway? In ten or fifteen years when her looks were gone, what would be left?

I chewed it over in my mind, and stared at myself a little longer. I went to bed feeling better. The thing I really needed to do was stop talking to her at all; sever all contact. I had sworn to do that several times in the past, but this time was different. I wasn't going to stop because it was unfair to Amber; I was doing it because it was unfair to me. As bad as that sounded, it was true. MaryAnn was simply a distraction. She wasn't worth the drama anymore.

That next evening, one of Amber's friends from high school was having a bachelorette party. Normally I would have hooked up with MaryAnn, but I wasn't even mildly tempted. There were a few NBA games on TNT so I called me brother to see if we could hook up.

"Hey," I said once he picked up, "you want me to pick up a twelve? Lakers are playing San Antonio."

"Can't tonight," he said.

Rob was a big Spurs fan, and he'd been merciless when they were killing the Lakers. I've loved the Lakers since the Showtime days so now that the roles had been reversed I was exacting my revenge.

"You not wanting to watch Kobe make little Timmy cry?" I asked.

"Actually," he said, a little smug, "I have a date tonight."

I laughed. "I'm supposed to buy that?"

"It's so hard to believe?"

"Was it a girl you met at the pawn shop, some chick who came in looking to buy a set of false teeth?"

"No, it wasn't a girl I met at the pawn shop," he mimicked. "I'm going out with Amanda."

"The dog-walker girl?" I asked. "Sorry, bro, but meeting her at the park so you can walk your dogs together isn't a date."

"You're a jackass," he said. "For your information, she's on her way over now with Chinese food, and we're going to watch a movie."

"Does she work at the Chinese place part-time?"

The next thing I heard was a dial tone. "I'm going to my brother's," I said to Amber, grabbing my coat.

"Is everything okay?"

I grinned. "Rob has a date. It's time for a little payback."

"You both need to grow up."

I took my time getting to his apartment and sat in the parking lot, the car in idle, until I saw Amanda pull up. She was carrying a paper bag in one hand and a DVD in the other. I quickly got out of the car.

"Here, let me help," I said, opening the door to the building.

"Thanks," she said, giving me a smile.

She walked up the stairs to Rob's apartment, me a few steps behind. We got to the door, and she looked at me, curiosity mixed with maybe a little fear.

"Are you coming over to visit Rob?" I asked, and she nodded. "I don't know if you remember me, but I'm his brother."

There was a spark of recognition. "Dallas, right?"

"It's Houston, but you're in the right state."

That generated a laugh. "What movie did you bring?" I asked.

She put the DVD cover face-up. "Oh, wow," I said. "P.S. I Love you. That's a fantastic movie. It's one of Rob's favorites."

She frowned. "He said he's never seen it before."

I tilted my head. "I always get those movies confused. Is that the one with all the different storylines that come together at the end? One guy's a prime minister, another one had a wife that died; I can't remember the rest."

"No, that's Love Actually."

I pressed a palm against my forehead. "That's it. Sorry, I get all those movies confused. I'm not nearly as into romantic movies as Rob."

She started to knock, but I stopped her. "I got it," I said.

Rob was in the kitchen lighting candles when we walked through the door. The smile on his face disappeared when he saw me.

"What are you doing here?" he asked.

I looked at the dog-walker girl and then back at Rob. "Are you talking to her or me?" I asked.

He stared at me for a long moment. "What are you doing here?" he asked through clinched teeth.

"I was in the neighborhood," I said innocently. "I thought we could watch the game."

If looks could kill, I would be a wet spot on the ground. "Well, now you know."

I looked over. "I'm sorry," I said to the dog-walker girl as I extended my hand. "You didn't tell me your name."

"Amanda," she said, shaking it.

"Wow," I said, taking a step back to look her over, "so you're the girl Rob talks about nonstop."

He tried to laugh, but it came out more as a cough. "That's not true," he said.

"Are you kidding?" I asked incredulously. "Ever since you saw her in the park you've barely talked about anything else."

I touched her shoulder. "I can only hope that someone loves me that much some day."

She looked at Rob, her eyes crinkling, and I let the silence linger for a few seconds. "I didn't mean to intrude, Amanda," I said. "Maybe I'll see you later."

I started for the door, and stopped as I grabbed the door handle. "Wait, are you the girl I sometimes see walking dogs?"

"Yeah," she said, still looking at Rob out of the corner of her eye.

"Quick question: if I bought a dog, would you be willing to walk him for me."

"I guess."

"The thing is, I would need to have him walked early in the morning."

She frowned. "Sorry, I work at the Java Joint from seven until noon."

"I drive past there every morning," I said. "I usually make my own, but a girl like you could make a guy throw away his coffee-maker just for an excuse to see you every day."

I opened the door. "Maybe you can double date with me and my girlfriend sometime," I offered.

"Maybe," she said, looking at Rob then back at me.

I gave her a wink. "Welcome to the family," I said on my way out the door.

I was brushing my teeth that night when the phone rang. "It's Rob," Amber called out.

I spit in the sink, then rinsed my mouth and spit again before I grabbed the phone. "Lakers won by ten," I said.

"You're an asshole."

"It was close until the last minute," I said.

"I can't believe you did that."

"What did I do?" I asked innocently.

"She said I was moving too fast and that she wasn't ready for that kind of relationship. She's not even going to walk the dog anymore."

I knew I had pushed it, but obviously I'd taken things too far. "I'll fix it," I said. "Honest to God, I didn't think that would happen."

"No, no, no," he said quickly. "All you'll do is make things worse."

"How can it get worse than refusing to even walk your dog? Like I said, I'll fix it."

The next day I stopped at the Java Joint on my way to the office. Amanda was working the register, and once she recognized me she refused to make eye contact.

"Hey, can I talk to you?" I asked.

"We're kind of busy," she said even though there was no one else in line.

"It'll only take a minute, I promise."

She finally looked up. "Last night I was a complete and utter jerk," I said. "Rob said he had a girl over and I was just trying to mess with him. Seriously, I just took things too far."

"No problem."

"See, you say that, but I think you're just patronizing me."

"I have a lot of things to do," she said, turning toward the back room.

"I know you're trying to get rid of me, but I'm not going anywhere until you hear me out," I said, raising my voice.

She stopped and slowly turned. "One minute."

"First, I'm sorry. I know the things I said made you uncomfortable, but all I was trying to do was piss him off and make him look like an ass."

"It worked."

I paused. "If it worked, then that means you believe it's my fault, not his, right?"

She clicked her teeth a few times, studying me. "Does he really like romantic movies?" she asked.

I looked at her for a long moment. "Not really, but honestly neither do I. Like I said, I'm the jerk, not him."

"Did he buy that dog just to meet me?"

I cleared my throat. "Why would you think that?"

"It's obvious he's not a dog lover, and there's no way he's owned that dog for more than a few months."

"He liked dogs when he was a kid," I lied. "Maybe seeing you was the thing that motivated him to do it, but he's wanted a dog for a long time."

"Did he ask you to come?" she asked.

"I swear to God he didn't," I said, raising my right hand. "In fact, he tried to stop me."

"So what if I tell you that your brother isn't my type?"

I thought about it. "Then I'd say I wasted the nice lady's time."

"You're wasting my time," she said. "He's not my type."

I stared at her for a few seconds before she looked away. "I know you don't know me from Adam, and I don't have any business asking you for a favor, but I'm going to anyway," I said. "Will you just go out with him a few times? Rob's my best friend, and if you don't he'll never forgive me."

She looked at me like she was considering. "I'll even…" I started, but then stopped.

"You'll even what?" she prodded.

"I was about to say I'd pay you, but then I realized what that sounds like. What if I get on my knees and beg? Would that work?"

Three middle-aged women chose that moment to walk through the front door, so I got on my knees and clasped my hands together. "Please say yes," I said, raising my voice.

The women started clapping and she turned red. "I'm not getting up until you say 'yes,'" I said.

"Okay, fine," she said through her teeth, her eyes darting to the women who were still standing in the doorway. "Now please stand up."

"If I tell him to give you a call you'll go out with him?"

"Fine."

"And you'll keep walking his dog?"

She hesitated and I clasped my hands together again from my position on the floor. "Please say yes," I said again. This generated an "Aww" from the women.

"I'll promise, but only if you swear not to get on your knees again."

"That's what she said."

She tilted her head. "What?"

"Never mind, bad joke. So if I tell him I talked to you, and you want to see him again, and he calls you'll go out with him?"

She sighed. "Okay."

I turned. "Sorry, ladies. I know I've monopolized this pretty girl's time, so to make up for it I'm going to buy your coffee."

"Thank you," they said in unison.

"In fact, if she agrees to go out with him three more times, I'll buy you a pastry, too."

The women looked back and forth between each other, me, and Amanda. "You're not getting married?" one of them asked.

I shook my head. "I've only met her once before," I said, taking a twenty from my wallet. I turned to Amanda. "Rob's a really good guy. I make him sound like my retarded older brother, but I guarantee you'll have a good time."

She didn't look convinced. "If you say so."

Chapter 11

I called Rob at the pawn shop, and after telling me I was an idiot and a jerk, he agreed to call. That evening he stopped by the apartment.

"You're the man," he said, special emphasis on "the man" as he gave me a hug and swung me around.

"That good, huh?" I asked once he put me down.

"We're going out tonight, she said to pick somewhere nice."

"So did you make the reservation at Applebee's or Chili's?"

He laughed. "Tonight I'll pretend to enjoy your snide little comments no matter how idiotic they are."

"Well, I'm glad she came around."

"Thanks," he said, his face getting serious. "No kidding. This makes up for last night."

"We're good?"

He nodded. "We're good."

"What did you do?" Amber asked after Rob had left.

"I broke it. It was my job to fix it."

"Is that what you do when you really screw things up?" she asked, laughing. "You pick up all the tiny pieces and glue them back together?"

I shrugged. "Sometimes it works better than others."

The next day on my lunch break I drove to a payphone and dialed MaryAnn's number.

"How you doing?" I asked when she picked up.

"I just tried calling you," she said. "Are you going to leave your little girlfriend tonight and come over?"

"Actually, that's what I wanted to talk to you about."

There were a few moments of dead air. "Okay," she said, more as a question.

"I don't think we should see each other anymore."

She sighed. "Another attack of conscience."

"I can't keep doing this to Amber. We're through."

"Houston, you have a problem." She always said that when she wanted to piss me off.

"You're right. And my problem is you. The way I see it, no more MaryAnn, no more problem."

"You'll come back," she said, sounding confident.

"Don't beg and plead, Mar. It's not your style." I smiled, knowing that one would get her.

"Me? Beg you? Oh my God," she said, drawing out each word.

"Take care, MaryAnn."

She was saying something else, but I hung up the phone. I almost skipped back to my car. It felt good being the one who broke it off, instead of the other way around. That feeling lasted until I got back to my desk.

"Have a nice lunch?" Dave asked as I sat down. His voice had raised a few octaves, and I glanced over at him out of the side of my eye. He was still my neighbor, and I was still working hard at my job in an attempt to avoid conversation.

"Yeah, it was all right," I said, punching my password into the computer.

"Some girl called. Said to call her back, you'd know the number."

An unmistakable challenge in his voice this time. "Okay," I said. "Thanks."

"Are you still dating Amber?"

I turned around. "What's your point?"

He stood up. "You messing around on her?" he asked, puffing out his chest.

"So what if I am?"

"You tell her the truth, or I will," he said, taking a menacing step forward.

"You really need to find a hobby and leave us alone."

"She's a nice girl."

I leaned toward him. "The reason you're so wound up is that you need to get laid," I whispered, reaching toward my back pocket for my wallet. "Since you'll probably have to pay for it, I'll help out with a donation."

The Amateur

Sure enough, he balled up his fist and swung at my head. I was ready for it, ducked under his arm, and then slammed him to the ground. We started rolling around on the floor, neither of us landing any punches; more just grappling and turning each other over. I looked up to see what seemed like the entire office watching us go at it. My manager, all five feet or so of her, waded in and separated us.

"This is a place of business," she said, talking like we were a couple kids on the playground. "Until security arrives, you sit here," she said, pointing at Dave and then at his desk. "And you sit there."

She pointed at me, then her office. Dave and I stared at each other a little longer, and then followed orders. Security arrived a few minutes later and I was ushered into a small office with a desk and three chairs. The place had the feel of an interrogation room. The only thing missing was a single light bulb hanging from the ceiling.

Shortly afterward, two guys walked in wearing off-the-rack black suits, and one shut the door. One was white and the other was black, but except for that minor detail they could have passed for twins. Both looked like ex-football players, and they each were glaring at me like I'd been a very bad boy.

The black guy walked around the desk and took a seat, while the white guy chose the chair next to me. Nothing was said for a while as we all looked back and forth at one another. I figured I'd start off with a joke, something to lighten the tension.

"Hey, guys," I said. "If this is about the extra five minutes I took on my lunch yesterday, I was fully intending to update that on my timecard." Maybe it wasn't the funniest joke in the world, but you'd have thought I was speaking a foreign language.

"Mr. Houston," the white guy said, looking down at a clipboard he was holding, "what is your explanation for what happened this afternoon?"

"Actually, my name is Houston Thomas, so it would be Mr. Thomas instead of Mr. Houston."

He gave me a deadpan stare.

"Not important," I said, clearing my throat. The way there were seated, I had to turn my head ninety degrees to look from one to the other.

"Anyway, this afternoon," I said, trying to match their scowls. "I came back from lunch when this guy, Dave, asks me a question. I told him it was none of his business and he tackled me. Next thing I knew someone was pulling us apart."

"What did he ask?" the black guy asked.

I turned in my chair so I could look at him. "He asked if I was cheating on my girlfriend."

"And why would he do that?" he asked, a curious frown on his face.

I shrugged. "Probably because she used to be his girlfriend."

They both finally smiled. "I see," said the black guy.

"He had a hard time accepting the fact that she chose me over him," I explained. "For the last month, he's been asking me questions about our relationship, and I've tried my best to be nice, but I guess he finally went over the edge."

"Did you say anything to provoke him, Mr. Houston?" the white guy asked.

I thought about correcting him again, but let it go. "He asked if I was messing around on her, and I said it was none of his business. There were probably three or four people who heard us talking, and I'm sure they'll tell you the same thing."

They looked at me for a little while longer, acting like they didn't believe me. Maybe they figured if they stared at me long enough I'd crack and make some kind of confession.

"We're going to talk to Mr. Wesselman and see how his story compares to yours," the black guy said right before they walked out.

Somewhere in the neighborhood of fifteen minutes passed before they returned. After they'd taken their seats they went back to staring at me. Another minute or so rolled by with none of us saying anything. That may not sound like a very long time, but when you have two big guys looking at you like you just insulted their' mothers it seems like an eternity.

"Mr. Wesselman's description of what happened is a lot different than yours," the black guy finally said.

"I'm telling you, ask the people who were sitting in our area. I have no idea what he told you, but what I said is the truth. He's still hung up on my girlfriend, and he blames me that they're not still together."

"He says that you told him that he would need to pay money in order to…," the black guy consulted his notepad, "'get laid.'"

I put up an arm and shrugged. "The guy's lying. All I told him was to leave me alone."

The white guy cleared his throat so I swiveled around to face him. "You said before that you told him to mind his own business. Did you tell him to leave you alone, or to mind his own business?"

"What's the difference?" I asked, my voice going up a few notches. "At different times I've told him both."

"And why do you think he didn't initiate a confrontation until now?"

I wanted to scream. "How should I know?"

They went back to staring at me. Finally, I couldn't take it anymore. "Look, if you want me to answer the same questions over and over again that's fine. I'm not saying you should believe me because I'm a good boy who doesn't lie. The only thing I'm asking you to do is talk to the people who were there."

They exchanged looks back and forth, and after a few seconds, the black guy gave a small, almost imperceptible nod, and they started toward the door.

"How much longer do I have to sit in this room?" I asked.

The white guy smiled. "Until I say you can leave."

Another ten minutes or so went by and finally my manager, Dawn, walked in. "Come with me," she said. Usually she and I had a good relationship, but she didn't even look back as I followed her out of the room.

"Where are we going?" I asked.

"Steve's office," she said without turning around.

Steve was the director of the department, and he didn't like me very much. He was a tall guy, and even though he looked like he was in good shape, he wasn't much of an athlete. The company had a flag football tournament every year, and our teams were matched up against each other a few years earlier. He was stuck defending me, and I scored three touchdowns in my team's first three possessions. That would have been bad enough, but I proceeded to run my mouth.

After my second touchdown, I yelled to his team, "You fellas better get someone else out here because this guy can't stop me."

Needless to say, things were strained between us after that point. Steve's office was definitely not the place I wanted to go.

Steve was sitting at his desk when we arrived, and I took a seat in the chair facing him. Dawn lingered for a moment before she walked out and closed the door.

He looked at me with a small smile. "It appears someone hasn't been playing well with others, Houston."

At this point I was ticked off. "It wasn't my fault. The guy threw a punch at me, and then tackled me. All I did was tell him that something was none of his business."

"His story is a little different."

"Did you ask the people who saw it? Ask them what happened. I didn't do anything."

He squinted his eyes, and gave me a pained expression. "I'm sorry, Houston, but we're going to have to let you go."

I was incredulous. "Even though it wasn't my fault?"

"Reliable has a zero-tolerance policy. Anyone who gets in a fight on company property is automatically let go. It doesn't matter who initiated it."

"But I didn't do anything."

"We have a zero-tolerance policy. I'm sorry." The smile on his face told a different story.

"So what you're saying is that if I come over that desk, even if I admit that I was completely to blame, we'd both get fired?"

The smile disappeared. "That would be different."

"I say we find out," I said. I made a move like I was going to go at him, and he jerked backward in his chair, then quickly grabbed his desk phone.

"Can you get security in here pronto?" he asked, then to me. "They'll escort you out."

"I can't go back and get my stuff?"

The smile returned. "It'll be mailed to you in the next few days."

A few seconds later, there was a knock on the door, and the same two security guards walked in. I got up and started following them, but then turned toward Steve. He had gotten out of his chair and was circling around his desk when we made eye contact.

"I guess you're happy that you won't have to guard me next year, huh?"

His eyes narrowed, but he didn't say anything. "Three touchdowns," I said, holding up three fingers. "Three."

Then as they grabbed my arms and steered me out, I leaned into his office. "Three touchdowns," I yelled, loud enough for everyone on the floor to hear.

"What was the point in asking me questions if I was going to be fired anyway?" I asked the security guards as they were guiding me down the stairs. They ignored me which pissed me off even more. "Is it okay if I call you guys Mumbo and Jumbo?"

"In a few seconds you can say whatever you want," the white guy grunted.

"So if I asked which of you was the top and which one was the bottom what kind of response would I get?" I asked.

They both came to a sudden halt. "You got a real smart mouth," said the black guy. He let go of my arm and I could tell he was waiting for me to take a swing. I was mad, but I wasn't stupid.

"He's not worth it," said the white guy even though he had turned three shades of red. The black guy grabbed my other arm and squeezed it a little harder. I was literally off the ground as they carried me the rest of the way down the stairs. At least five or six people passed me on their way from the cafeteria.

"Hey, Ryan," I said to a guy who was on my old team, "these guys are gay for each other." He just looked at me like I was crazy, and continued walking.

The white guy dug his thumb in my elbow, making my whole arm go numb. "What did he tell you about running your mouth?" he asked.

"You're a real brave guy, saying that to someone with his arms held."

They used my forehead to open the building's entrance door, and then bodily threw me out onto the sidewalk where I landed on my hip and shoulder.

"You got ten minutes to get off company property before we arrest you for trespassing," the black guy said.

"You timing me, asshole?" I asked from a sitting position on the ground.

They looked at each other, and the white guy shook his head and both walked back inside. I was tempted to wait for Dave so we could have another go, but figured what would be the point? Instead, I drove home and waited for Amber. It was a little after one when I got there, but I knew once she heard the news she'd come straight home. Sure enough, she arrived about twenty minutes later.

"What happened?" she asked the moment she walked through the door.

I shrugged, trying to look innocent. "The guy attacked me. He said something about me lying about having a fiancé and before I knew it, we were rolling around on the floor."

She looked mystified. "And they fired you for that?"

"They said something about a zero-tolerance policy. I don't understand it either."

She sat down and covered her head with her hands. "This is my fault."

"The guy's crazy. That's hardly your fault."

"Did they say anything else?"

I shrugged. "Just that they'll mail my things."

"I'm so sorry, sweetie," she said, giving me a hug.

"I just wish I understood what happened," I said, milking it. "One minute I'm sitting there minding my own business, the next he calls me an asshole and throws a punch at me." It was kind of true.

The good thing about working in customer service was that you don't have to worry about staying unemployed for long, so I knew it wouldn't be tough finding another job. That could change, though, if the new company found out that there had been a fight at my previous employer.

"Do you think this will go on my record?" I asked.

She looked like she was considering it for the first time. "I'm sure my stepdad will know."

I was still playing the role of martyr when we went to have dinner with her family that evening. Amber told them about, as she termed it, my unfortunate situation. She mentioned the thing about my record, and her stepfather looked at me thoughtfully.

"I have a lot of people I can put you in contact with," he said, rubbing his chin. "It might be a little different than the type of work you're used to, but the pay is probably as good or better, and it'll give you great benefits."

I tried to act intrigued, but there was a reason I'd chosen white-collar over blue-collar. Working outside digging ditches in sub-zero temperature wasn't my idea of making a living.

"Come by the plant tomorrow and I'll see what we can do. With your education, we may be able to find some kind of accounting position. Does eight o'clock work for you?"

My ears perked up. Maybe digging ditches wasn't the type of work he had in mind. "I'll be there," I said.

The next day, I arrived about fifteen minutes early. Instead of making me wait like people in the finance industry love to do, the lady in the office started showing me around right away. She was kind of cute in a trashy way; bleached-blonde hair that was showing dark roots, but an incredible body.

She gave me a tour of the entire plant, and told me that my job would primarily consist of punching purchase orders into the computer, and making a few calculations that required basic math. If things were slow, I would also do some light clerical work.

Amber's stepfather came in a few minutes later with a big smile. "So what do you think?"

"When do I start?"

He laughed. "There are still a few things left to do," he said, then paused. "You'll need to take a drug test. Will that be a problem?"

"No, absolutely not."

He looked relieved. "Glad to hear it. I'll have Tonya here take you over so you can get it all done." He nodded at her and walked away.

"He really seems to like you," she said.

"I guess," I said, trying to look sheepish. I started to say something about dating his stepdaughter, but reconsidered. "How long will this take?"

"Only half an hour or so to fill out the paperwork, but you'll need to go to St. Luke West for the drug test. If everything checks out, you'll probably start on Monday."

"Great," I said. "Are we going to be in the same office?"

She stopped and looked at me, studying me a little. "Yes we will."

"Great," I said again. "It'll be nice to have someone to show me around."

"You've already seen everything," she said, giving me a small smile. Obviously she knew when a man was hitting on her. I held her eyes for a few beats longer than was probably appropriate.

"So you work here long?" I asked.

She shrugged. "A year or so."

"Your boyfriend, husband, or whatever, does he work in the plant?"

Her eyes narrowed, and she smiled. We were definitely flirting. "No."

"You mind me asking where he works?"

"What about you? Where does your girlfriend work?"

She had me there. No doubt word would leak around the plant that I was dating the union leader's daughter.

"Reliable Investments," I said. "I actually worked there at one point, but things didn't work out."

"My husband," she said, putting special emphasis on the word 'husband,' "works in a different plant."

She handed me a stack of forms, comprised of four pages that needed my signature, and a place asking for my name and personal information. I always cringe when I get one of those, because I know best-case scenario that I'll get an odd look. I filled it out and handed it back to her.

"Is your first name Houston?" she asked.

I nodded. "As in 'Houston, we have a problem?'" she said, sounding like she was speaking into a microphone.

"Yeah, one and the same."

"I bet you get that a lot, huh?"

"Only once before." I'm sure the sarcasm must have come through in my tone.

She looked at me for a long moment, but didn't say anything else. I drove over to the hospital for my drug test, the whole time wondering why I couldn't stop looking at other girls. I hadn't done it with MaryAnn. Why was I doing it now? I needed to find the closest bathroom and give myself a talk in the mirror.

The thing about Tonya was that she wasn't all that attractive. She had a great body, but no lips to speak of, and a dead tooth that was like a homing beacon.

It was a little after one when I got out of the hospital, and I drove straight home. I had really wanted coffee, but there was a chance that MaryAnn was at Starbucks. It was a risk not worth taking.

The next few days were relaxing. I had forgotten how nice it was not to set the alarm. All my paperwork had been approved and I was definitely starting on Monday of the following week. Honestly, I would have been happy to get another week off. I had a week of vacation left from Reliable, but I figured it would sound ungrateful to bring it up.

I wanted to do something for the weekend; something like travel outside the city and stay in a hotel. On Friday, I mentioned it to Amber, and she liked the idea.

We were packing on Friday night around six when the phone rang. Amber answered it, as I continued to put things in a suitcase.

"Hello," she said distractedly, packing her things together. All of a sudden, she stood straight up and her eyes widened.

"It's Dave," she whispered, covering the mouthpiece. "What do you want?" she asked him.

I pretended to stay busy, but I was watching for her reaction. "Uh huh," she said, and then a few seconds later. "Uh huh."

She was looking out the window, in the opposite direction of where I stood. "Is that right?" followed by, "Well, what if I don't believe you?"

Then, "No you didn't, but…"

She then turned her eyes on me. I tried to look curious, but not worried. "Why should I believe you?" she asked him.

"What's he saying?" I asked.

She didn't cover the mouthpiece this time. "He said that the reason he tried to hit you is because you cheated on me."

She didn't look like she was convinced either way. "That's ridiculous," I said, reaching for the phone. She pulled away a little.

"He also says that there's a girl who called you all the time."

I shook my head. "The only girls who called were my mom and sisters. Give it to me," I said again, pointing at the phone. This time after a brief hesitation she handed it over.

"Hey, Dave," I said. "I don't exactly what you're trying to prove here, but all you're doing is making an even bigger ass of yourself than you did before."

"I'm just telling Amber the truth."

"What are you trying to get out of this? You trying to get Amber to meet you again? Do you need more closure?"

"She's a nice girl. She deserves a lot better than you."

"You mean like you? Listen, pal, there's a message everyone else can see that's obviously going over your head. She dumped you, dude, and I had nothing to do with it."

Amber reached for the phone, but I pushed her hand away. "Listen carefully," I said, drawing out each word. "She dumped you. Get used to it, get over it, get on with it."

"Give it to me," Amber whispered. I held up a finger.

"Houston, you have a problem," he said. If I could have, I would have reached through the phone.

"You think you're the first person to use that line? You're an idiot."

"She can do a lot better than you."

"You're right. She could probably do better than me, but I got news for you, buddy. You ain't it."

Amber reached for the phone again and this time I let her take it. "Dave, you shouldn't do this to yourself. It's bad enough that you got Houston fired, but…"

She listened for a moment. "Well, I'm sorry to hear that, but it doesn't change anything." Then, "Did you see him cheat on me?" A few seconds later, "he said it was his mother or sisters."

This time longer, "You're not making sense. Why would he admit it to you?"

"Dave, Dave," she said, apparently interrupting him. "Listen to me, okay? Don't call here anymore."

Interrupting again, "I don't care. I'm done listening. Goodbye."

Except she didn't hang up the phone. Why do women do that? She listened a little longer, then said, "I don't…" before I pulled the phone away from her.

"She said she's done listening, asshole," I said and then slammed down the receiver.

"That went well," I said.

She looked at me like she still wasn't convinced. "He said you admitted that you cheated on me."

I rolled my eyes. "Come on. Is he my freakin' therapist? I did everything I could do to avoid the guy, and I'm going to make a confession? Does he think he's a priest?"

She seemed to relax. "You're right," she said, starting to pack again. "I know you're right."

"This is just his way of trying to see you again."

She zipped up her suitcase and put it against the wall. "You're not going to go looking for him, are you?"

"Why, so I can give him another excuse to call?"

That was the end of the conversation.

Chapter 12

We mutually decided on West Virginia as a destination for our trip, and the weekend was a lot of fun. The only bad part, and the reason I would never return, was zigzagging up and down hills on the expressway with trucks right on my bumper.

We stayed in Bentley, which was smack dab in the middle of nowhere. The plan when we set out was to just cross over the state line, but a helpful gas station attendant said something about a bridge that was the only one of its kind.

Like fools we decided to check it out. It was a nice bridge, but hardly worth the extra four-hour drive. Amber fell asleep about two hours from home, and as I listened to the radio I found myself thinking about my new job.

I usually make a good impression when I start, but then I tend to run off at the mouth. I vowed this time to keep my mouth shut and try to fit in, but that was easier said than done. I hadn't done a very good job keeping my vows. We got in around ten in the evening, and Amber woke up right about the time I pulled into the parking lot.

The next morning, I set the alarm for six-thirty to make sure I arrived at work on time. The last thing I wanted was to be late the first day.

I got there about a half-hour early which gave me plenty of time to get settled. Amber's step-dad stopped by around noon to see how things were going, and was surprised that I'd already figured out what I was supposed to do. It wasn't difficult, just punching data into a computer. In all honesty, you could probably train a monkey to do it in no time at all.

I left for the day around 5:00 and when I got to the apartment, Amber was making dinner.

"How was your first day?" she called out.

I hung up my coat in the closet and then walked up behind her. "You should quit Reliable and go work for your stepdad," I said, putting my arms around her waist.

"That good?"

"But only if he doesn't give you my job."

She wiped her hands on a towel, then turned and gave me a kiss. "Dinner will be ready in about twenty minutes."

I went to the living room and turned on the television. Another of the many things I loved about Amber was that everything wasn't a contest. With MaryAnn, she had a mental ledger and if she thought she was doing more work than me she would refuse to do anything else until I caught up. I was still on the couch watching Sportscenter and about half way through dinner when the phone rang.

"It's your brother," Amber yelled from the kitchen.

"Tell him I'll call him back," I said through a mouthful of food.

A few seconds later she carried the phone into the living room. "He said it's important."

I put my plate on the coffee table and wiped my hands on my pants. "Somebody better be dead," I said, after picking up the receiver.

"You're an ungrateful prick," he said. "MaryAnn is on her way over and she sounds seriously pissed."

Amber was standing a few feet away, trying to snoop without being obvious, but failing miserably. "She say what she wants?" I asked.

"All I know is that she was pissed, but she's always sounded like that when she was talking to me."

"Did MaryAnn give you a number where I can reach her?"

There was a pause. "You're doing that for Amber's benefit, right?"

"Give me a second. Let me grab a pen."

"You know I don't have the number, right?"

Amber handed me a pen from her purse. "Okay, go ahead."

"It's 1-800-you owe me a twelve-pack."

I wrote down MaryAnn's number. "Okay, thanks. And you'll have to fill me in on how things are going at the pawn shop next time I see you."

I hung up before he could say anything else. "Was that about your ex-girlfriend?" Amber asked, and I nodded. "Did she say what she wants?"

"No idea, but Rob said it was important. Are you okay with me calling her from here?"

"What do you think it's about?"

"With her it could be anything."

It was only ten or so miles from her place to Rob's apartment so I knew if MaryAnn wasn't there already she would be there soon.

I quickly dialed her number. "Hey, it's Houston," I said when she answered.

"Where are you?" she snapped.

I gave a sideways glance at Amber. "I'm living with Amber. I thought you knew that."

"Give me the address."

I snorted. "I'm not giving you the address to my girlfriend's apartment."

"Give me the damn address," she said, screaming now.

"You need to calm down and tell me what this is about."

There was a delay of a few seconds. "Did you put a private investigator on me?"

"An investigator? Why would I do that?"

"Answer the question. Did you put a private investigator on me?"

My first thought was that it might be Amber so I looked straight at here when I answered, scanning her face for a reaction. "I could care less what you do or who you see. Why would I put an investigator on you?"

Amber looked mystified which made me feel better.

"Well somebody did," MaryAnn said.

"I don't know what you want me to do about it. You're not my problem anymore."

Another pause. "I don't believe you."

"I don't really care what you do or don't believe," I said, raising my voice to match hers. "It's not me, I don't know who it is, and I have no idea why."

Amber was poking me. "Hold on a second," I said to MaryAnn, and then covered the mouthpiece.

"Maybe you should have her come over," Amber said.

"Hell no," I whispered. "If she knows where we live, she'd be over here every time she has a problem."

"Hello," MaryAnn said, drawing out the word.

I uncovered the mouthpiece. "Give me a second."

"You're using up all my minutes."

"The longer you keep talking, the longer it's going to take and the more minutes you're going to use up."

"Call me back when you figure it out," she said. The next thing I heard was a click.

I looked at Amber. "I'll meet her somewhere if you're okay with it, but there's no way in hell she's coming here."

Her eyes went to the ground. "Do you want to see her again?"

I pulled her close, and she put her head against my chest. "The only way I'll meet her is if you're totally okay with it."

She looked up and smiled, a sad smile. "I trust you."

I was a complete and utter jerk, no doubt about it. I called MaryAnn back.

"You finally figured it out?" she asked.

"Stop it with the attitude. I'll meet you somewhere if it's that important, but there's no way you're coming here."

"Does your girlfriend know you were with me less than a week ago?"

Amber was standing less than five feet away, and I prayed she hadn't heard. "Do you want to meet or what?"

"Rock Bottom?" she asked, laughing.

"I'll meet you at the Chili's a few blocks from our old apartment," I said. "I'll be there in twenty minutes. If you're not in the parking lot when I show up then you can figure it out on your own."

"You are such a drama queen. See you in twenty minutes."

"You're more than welcome to come with me," I said to Amber after I disconnected. I only offered because I knew she would turn it down.

"Am I the one you want to be with?" she asked in a small voice.

I kissed the top of her head and then a couple other places on the way down to her mouth. "I want to spend the rest of my life with you."

It surprised me when I said it, but it was one-hundred percent true. Amber smiled and gave me a peck on the cheek.

"Maybe we can do something when you get home," she said.

I got in the car and drove the ten- or so miles to the restaurant. MaryAnn was standing next to the entrance holding a black disk about the size of a coaster when I pulled into the parking lot. As I walked up, she looked at her watch.

"I was about to leave," she said. I was less than five minutes late.

"Then it's a good thing for you I got here when I did. Did you get us a table?"

"She said it'll only be a couple more minutes," MaryAnn said. Maybe five seconds later, the coaster-looking thing lit up like a Christmas tree. The hostess led us to a booth in the back corner of the restaurant.

"What are you talking about with the private investigator and why do you think I'm involved?" I asked once we were seated.

Her eyes narrowed. "It had to be you or your girlfriend. This creep was following me around so I called the police and told them someone was stalking me. They called me back and said it was some private detective, and he promised to leave me alone. Then today the asshole calls and asks if I'm still seeing you, when was the last time I was with you, and if I'm still in love with you."

I felt a chill. "What did you say?"

"I told him to go to hell and leave me alone."

"Why would you think it was me?" I asked. "I already know the answer to all those questions."

"Please. You know good and well you want to know if I'm still in love with you."

I rolled my eyes. "Who broke it off? Why would I do that if I was worried about it?"

She studied me for a long moment. "You swear it wasn't you?"

I held up my right hand. "I swear," and then a few seconds later, "and it wasn't Amber, either."

"How can you say that for sure?"

"She said it wasn't her, and she's never lied to me."

MaryAnn laughed. "She would probably say the same thing about you."

"She's a better person than me."

She looked at me a little cock-eyed. "It sounds like you're in love with her. How could you be in love with her and sleeping with me at the same time?"

"Because I'm a self-centered prick."

Right about then the waitress walked up. "Can I get you guys something to drink?" she asked, her expression clearly showing she'd heard my last statement.

"Bud Light draft for me," I said. MaryAnn pointed at herself, then held up two fingers.

"Do you think it might be your boyfriend?" I asked once the waitress left.

"He doesn't even know your name."

I leaned back against the booth. "I have a hard time believing he doesn't know you were engaged to a guy named Houston."

"He thinks I haven't seen you for three months. I've dated two guys since you and he didn't mention either of them."

"Then I'm out of ideas."

She eyed me for a few seconds longer. "I still think it was you."

"Believe what you want, I could care less. Like I said, you're not my problem anymore."

The waitress arrived with our beers, and looked at me for a few beats. She was moderately attractive, about five-feet seven with straight blonde hair that was tied back in a ponytail and pale blue eyes. I gave her my best smile and touched her hand when she set the beer in front of me.

I looked at her nametag. "Thank you, Amanda," I said. "I'm sure you hear this a lot, but you have beautiful eyes."

"Thank you," she said. "I like yours, too."

I heard MaryAnn make a loud "huh" as I gave the waitress a wink. "I can't believe she flirted with you right in front of me," she said after the waitress walked away. "That was so rude."

I craned my neck so I could watch the waitress disappear around the corner before turning to MaryAnn. "I'm sorry, what did you say?" I asked, trying my best to hide a smile.

"I can't believe you."

I tilted my head thoughtfully. "I wonder if I should ask for her number."

"You're an asshole," she said.

"She was definitely interested. Did you see the way she looked at me?"

"You have a girlfriend."

"That never stopped me before," I said, getting to my feet. "I'll be right back."

I walked around the bar and to the bathroom. I knew MaryAnn would be going crazy. Other girls being interested in me always pissed her off.

I stayed for several minutes before returning to the table. "We're going out tomorrow night," I said after taking a long swallow of my beer. "That girl has a *serious* case of the hots for me."

"I'm out of here," she said, reaching for her purse. The waitress came back just as she was getting up.

"Are you ready to order?"

"I'm leaving," MaryAnn said, all attitude. "Houston, I'm sure your girlfriend is expecting you."

I winked at the waitress who smiled in return. "Could we get separate checks?" I asked.

"You're an asshole," MaryAnn said.

The waitress was looking back and forth between us, and I leaned toward her. "Sorry," I said in a conspirital whisper. "Jealous ex-girlfriend."

"Oh my God," MaryAnn said. "Look at me and look at you."

She threw a five-dollar bill on the table and stormed out of the restaurant.

"Is everything okay?" the waitress asked.

I over-tipped her with a ten and took a last swallow of my beer. "Sorry, she sometimes gets that way when she doesn't take her medication."

The Amateur

That generated the expected laugh, and I walked out to the parking lot. MaryAnn was standing next to my car, right leg cocked and arms crossed.

"I'm telling the police it was you if I ever see that guy again."

"Tell them what you want," I said, brushing her aside as I climbed in the car. "If you had half a brain in your head you'd try shaking down the agency where that guy worked instead of hassling me."

I left her chewing on that one as I drove away. About an hour after I got home, Amber and I went to Palomino for dinner and drinks, and then stopped at Blockbuster on our way to the apartment. We were somewhere in the neighborhood of an hour into the movie when the phone rang. Amber looked at me expectantly for a few seconds before I finally pushed myself off the couch to get it.

"Hello," I said.

There was a long pause. "Can I talk to Amber?" a male voice asked in a low falsetto.

"Hold on a second," I said, walking over and handing her the phone.

"Hello," she said, and then a few seconds later. "Dave?"

I ran into the bedroom and grabbed the other phone. "…around on you," was all I heard.

"What's he saying?" I asked.

"I have proof, asshole," he said. "I have pictures of you with another woman."

"You a graphic artist?" I asked, matching his tone. "The only way you have pictures is if you used Photoshop."

"I hired a private investigator, asshole."

"Why are you still bothering us, Dave?" Amber asked.

"I care about you," he said.

"Why don't you spend that money you're making washing dishes at Denny's buying yourself a girlfriend instead of hiring detectives."

"I'm making a lot more money than you," he said. "I got a job in corporate headquarters at Arby's."

"Dave, please leave me alone," Amber said quietly.

"He's a jerk," he said.

"I think your break's over," I said. "Go man the register before you get fired again."

"Houston, please let me handle this," Amber said.

"It sounds like he's trying to find a way to see you again," I said. "I think the poor fella needs more closure."

"You sure as hell better hope I never see *you* again," he said.

"I thought they taught you guys in the service industry that the customer is always right. Now shut your mouth, and go fetch me some curly fries, tough guy."

"Houston," Amber said, this time a lot louder. "Let me handle this."

"Sure, sweetie," I said, putting as much seduction in my voice as I could muster. "Come back to bed when you're done. You know I need your body heat to keep me warm."

He was yelling something else when I disconnected the line. Amber was still talking when I sat down beside her on the couch.

"Dave, you need to find a way to let this go," she said. "Instead of paying all that money to a detective you should get yourself a psychologist. Don't ever call here again."

He was still talking when she hung up. "What is it with that guy?" I asked.

"He said you brainwashed me."

I pulled her off the couch. "You want to go to bed with me," I said, looking into her eyes. "Resistance is futile."

She laughed. "You don't have to brainwash me for that."

The next day around 11 a.m. Amber called me at work. She had taken the day off, and I figured it was about meeting for lunch.

"What's up?" I asked, only half-listening as I read through a column by The Sports Guy on ESPN.com.

"Dave's on his way over with proof you cheated on me."

I stood up. "Right now?"

"He said he's bringing pictures."

I racked my brain, but I hadn't done anything with another girl since the incident at work. "I'm on my way," I said.

I yelled something to Tonya about a family emergency as I sprinted out the door and drove home. There was a midnight blue Ford

Mustang out front, a car I hadn't seen before and could only assume belonged to Dave. Our apartment was on the second floor and I was on my way up the stairs when I heard Amber's voice. I stopped about halfway up, only Dave's shoes visible.

"I knew he was there," Amber said. "I told him to go."

"I'm in love with you," he said, a little urgency in his voice. "Those months we spent together were the best months of my life. I know you love me, too, but this guy's fooled you into believing things that aren't true."

"I don't love you," she said. "In fact, right now I don't even like you very much."

"Promise you'll at least think about it?"

"Dave, you're scaring me," she said, her voice going up a few octaves.

I walked up the remaining stairs and saw Amber, eyes wide, her body wedged between the door and our apartment. Dave was only a few feet away. I could see the relief wash across her face like a wave as I approached. Dave turned and straightened, his hands clinching to fists.

"If you don't leave now I'm calling the police," Amber said, her voice like steel.

Dave looked like he was about to charge, but instead walked past me and down the stairs.

"Hey, Dave," I called out, "if you need more closure run into a door."

He stopped and glared at me for a long moment, and then continued out to the parking lot.

"You okay?" I asked Amber.

She shuddered. "I've never been happier seeing someone in my entire life than I was when you walked around that corner."

I led her to the couch. "You want something to drink?" I asked, and she shook her head.

I settled in next to her and she rested her head on my shoulder.

"What happened between you and that guy?" I asked.

"I wish I knew," she said with a shrug.

"It's been, what, nine months since you broke up?" I asked. "You must have really put it on him."

She slapped me and when I laughed she slapped me again.

"So, seriously, you never told me about that," I said. "What happened between you two?"

She stretched her arms across the top of the couch and looked skyward. "He asked me out at least five times before I finally said 'yes.' Things were okay at the beginning, but after we'd dated four or five months he started talking about forever. That really creeped me out, and I told him to slow down. A few weeks after that you and me had that talk on the trail. I already knew he wasn't the guy for me, but I didn't break up with him until that happened. When I told him I just wanted to be friends he freaked. He asked if it was to be with you and I said 'no.'"

I laughed. "At the time it was true," she said defensively.

"Do you think he's finally gotten the hint?"

"God, I hope so."

"If he comes over again call the police," I said, and she rolled her eyes. "I'm serious, the second you see him. Hiring an investigator to track down his ex-girlfriend's new boyfriend is crazy. Do you think he's got somebody trailing you, too?"

Her eyes widened. "Why would I think that?"

"He calls you at home on a day you're almost always at work? How does he know you'd be here?"

She shuddered. "That's creepy."

I looked at my watch. "I have to get back, but promise you'll call the police if he comes back."

I gave her a kiss and walked out to the car. I was reaching for the door handle when I saw Dave coming across the parking lot, walking fast.

"Why aren't you in your little uniform?" I asked, giving him an appraising look.

"I work in corporate, asshole," he said. He had approached from the passenger side, and my car was parked facing a six-feet tall retaining wall so the only way to get to me was from around the trunk.

"You and I both know you're cheating on Amber."

It was obvious he had some kind of recording device. "I'm completely devoted to Amber," I said, giving him an exaggerated wink. "I wouldn't even consider being with another girl."

"That's a lie."

"Here's something you might want to keep on your digital recorder. Amber thinks you're a creep and a stalker. She wanted me to make love to her after you left because she was so scared. She'll probably keep me up all night tonight."

His ears turned a pretty shade of pink. "I don't care about that. I just want to hear you admit you cheated on her."

"You sure are bossy for a guy who works at a fast-food restaurant. Now go get me some curly fries and a jamocha shake before I report you to your manager."

He came around the car in about four strides and hit me with a right that rocked me to my heels, then followed it up with a left that caught me right below the eye. I gave a tentative jab at his face with my left hand, and after slapping it aside, he hit me with another right. At that point, I put my head down and started swinging like a mad man.

"Stop it," Amber screamed. I looked up and took a straight right to the mouth for my trouble. Amber started hitting and pushing Dave. When he put his hands up to stop her I threw a roundhouse right with everything I had that caught him directly below the ear and he went down hard. I was about to kick him in the ribs when Amber shoved me in the chest.

"Do you want the neighbors to call the cops?" she asked. I thought about it for another second before taking a step back.

"That was a cheap shot," Dave said from his position on the ground. I snickered and he sprang to his feet like he was coming after me again.

"Get out of here," Amber screamed, pushing Dave's head with both hands. "I swear to God I'll call the cops if I ever see you again."

"And I'm still waiting on my curly fries," I chimed in.

"Shut up with the Arby's references already," Amber said.

Dave looked like he wanted to take another swing, but Amber positioned herself between us. He kept glaring at me the entire time he walked to his car.

Once he'd driven away, Amber slapped me hard on the arm. "You need to grow up," she said. "All that Arby's crap made everything a whole lot worse. It's no wonder he hates you."

"Sorry," I mumbled. I could taste the blood on my teeth, and my jaw hurt something fierce, but my hands were sore and my knuckles were scraped up so I knew I'd gotten in some good shots. I was prepared to call it a draw.

"God, you look horrible," she said, touching my face.

She led me to the bathroom and after I saw the robin's egg-sized bump on my cheekbone and my left eye which was almost swollen shut I thought maybe it wasn't even after all. The antibiotic ointment she put on my face hurt, and the ice stung at the beginning when she put it against my eye, but the washcloth that cleaned the blood from my split lip and sore hands felt pretty good.

"Promise you'll walk away if he comes after you again," she said.

I shook my head. "I can't do that. I'm not a runner."

She laughed. "Well, you're not much of a fighter. At least promise you'll stop with the Arby's crap."

"You sure are asking for a lot of promises," I said. She smiled and gave me a kiss that made me wince.

"What ticks me off the most is knowing that MaryAnn was right," I said. "It's my fault some idiot was following her around."

"Are you going to call her and apologize?" she asked, the little girl voice coming back.

"If I never see that girl again it will be too soon."

She pushed me softly in the chest. "Go back to work."

"You're okay?"

She nodded. "Let me know if my stepdad says anything."

"Swear you'll call the police if he comes back."

"You sure are asking me to swear on a lot of things."

I rolled my eyes and she started laughing. "I'll see you in a few hours," I said.

I stopped in the bathroom and inspected myself in the mirror. I still looked bad, but not nearly as much as I had twenty minutes earlier.

Dave's blue Mustang wasn't in the parking lot either at home or work. As I walked through the factory on the way to my office I received a few second glances. Tonya walked over as I was hanging up my coat.

"My God, what happened to you?"

I tried to look pissed off. "Some twelve-year old kid on a bike cut me off on my way back from lunch. That little guy could scrap."

She laughed. "A twelve-year old," she said, more statement than question.

"She might have kicked my ass, but I got the last laugh. That kid's hands are going to hurt for a week."

"You're a dork."

I shrugged. "What can I tell you? I'm more of a lover than a fighter."

"Judging from your face, you must be Casanova."

From that day forward, no one at work called me Houston.

Chapter 13

A month or so after I started at the plant, Amber took a different job at Reliable. It paid a lot more money, but instead of being a straight eight-thirty to five, she now had a wacky schedule where she worked three nights a week and every other Friday. It was a rough transition for both of us. Most of the nights Amber worked, I'd wile away the hours channel-surfing from a sprawled-out position on the couch.

Rob was spending practically every waking moment with the dog-walker girl, so I was surprised when he called one night and asked me to come over. There was an NBA double-header on TNT, and I figured we'd sit around watching the game, maybe making small conversation between commercials and drinking until the beer ran out.

We were sitting there, not really saying anything, when out of the blue, he said, "I want to talk to you about something."

I looked over, but he was still staring at the screen, a bland expression on his face. "It's about Amanda," he said.

"The dog-walker girl?"

"When are you going to stop calling her that?" he asked, facing me, an irritated expression on his face. "How hard is it to remember her name?"

"Tell you what," I said, getting up to grab another beer, "the day you put a ring on that girl's finger, I'll call her whatever you want."

"That's what I want to talk to you about," he said after a second or two. "I'm thinking about proposing."

I was reaching into the refrigerator, but stopped. "That's a joke, right?"

He didn't say anything. "You've been dating this girl for what, three months?" I asked.

"When you know, you know."

I handed him a beer. "You realize once you propose, you'll never see her again," I said, grunting as I sat down.

"What's that supposed to mean?" he asked, popping the top.

"It means she won't return your calls or answer the door. What do you think it means?"

He got quiet for a few seconds. "I love her," he mumbled.

"Jesus, Rob," I said, looking skyward. "You sure about this?"

"Never been more sure of anything in my life."

I shook my head. "I give you credit for balls. Whatever you do, don't act like you're going to break things off when you ask the girl. That would be a big mistake."

That got a laugh. "I'll remember that."

"You got the ring and everything?"

He nodded. "Was it something you got from the pawnshop, somebody sell it to you on the cheap?" I asked.

"No, I didn't get it at the pawnshop," he mimicked.

"You know how you're going to do it?"

He shrugged. "Drop down to one knee and say please."

"How can she resist a line like that?"

"If you can think of something better let me know."

"I think you're an idiot, but if she says 'yes' you get free dog-walking services for the rest of your life."

"I'll let you know how it goes," he said.

A few days later, Amber called out that my brother was on the phone.

"She shot me down," he said.

"I hate saying I told you so, but..."

He laughed. "I knew you didn't think I could pull it off. Actually, she said 'yes.' She even cried when I asked."

"Are you sure she knew you were proposing? Marry me sounds a lot like Tahiti."

"You're an idiot."

"Based on how you mumble, she might have thought you were asking her to go on a vacation."

"I was going to ask you to be my best man, jackass," he mumbled.

"Did you just ask me to go on a trip to Cancun?"

"The wedding is in June. Stop being an idiot and let me know if you'll do it or not."

"Unless she calls it off, I'll clear the entire month," I said, laughing. "Seriously, though, that's awesome. Sometimes I don't give you enough credit."

There was a pause. "Since we're being serious and all, I want to thank you. Amanda told me what happened at the coffee shop, and she said she never would have gone out with me again if it hadn't been for that."

"Like I said, it was my job to fix it. You don't owe me anything. That's what best friends do."

Amber was standing in the living room doorway, a faint smile touching her features.

I cleared my throat. "How about we agree not to talk this way again?"

"Okay, but no joke. This makes up for all the hell you've put me through the last thirty years."

"Then I guess the real question is how you're going to make up all the stuff you've done to me?"

There was a short pause. "Next time the Lakers play the Spurs, beers are on me."

I whistled. "Mr. Big Spender."

I hung up and saw Amber staring at me. "What?" I asked.

"The people who wonder what I see in you should hear what you just said."

"I broke it..." I started, but she interrupted.

"I know, it was your job to fix it," she said. "The way it sounds, you did a lot more than that."

She walked over and kissed me, and looked up as she put her arms around my waist. "You can be a jerk sometimes, but I know deep down you're a good guy."

"You sure about that?"

"Not a doubt in my mind."

For the most part, I figured it was true. The whole thing with MaryAnn was behind me, and that door had closed. There was no way I'd risk my relationship with Amber even if I knew I could get away with it. I made up my mind to appreciate her and be a committed boyfriend, someone she deserved.

That lasted until one Thursday morning. I was on my way to work when I saw a fire-engine red VW Bug sitting on the side of the road. Next to the driver's side door was a girl with shoulder-length auburn hair, her back to me. The road wasn't very busy, and it was cold, around twenty degrees.

I pulled onto the shoulder and walked back to her car. She watched as I approached, a leery expression on her face. She was about five-feet nine with a generous mouth, broad, upturned nose, wedge-shaped face, and large eyes the color of the Irish countryside. Taking her features individually, she wasn't very attractive; combine them all together, though, and she was breathtaking.

"You okay?" I asked.

She was talking on her cell phone, but clicked it close. "Flat tire," she said.

She followed me as I walked around to the back passenger side where I saw the rim grinding into the pavement.

"Houston," I said, turning and extending my hand.

She looked at me for a second before taking it. "Lauren."

"So, Lauren," I said, putting special emphasis on her name, "do you have a spare?"

She was still holding my right hand, but held up her phone with the other. "Thanks, but someone's coming."

She smiled, kind of an inviting smile, and I took a step forward. "So call them back."

We looked back and forth for a few seconds, and she finally shrugged. "Why not?"

Her trunk was already open, and I rolled up my sleeves before taking out the spare. I was jacking up the car when I heard her on the phone.

"Some nice guy stopped to help," A pause, and then, "he seems harmless."

I glanced up to see her watching me. After a second she smiled. "I'll be fine," she said, right before snapping the phone closed.

"Boyfriend?" I asked, pretending to focus on the tire.

She laughed. "My boyfriend would say you needed to get back in your car."

It took less than five minutes to change the tire, and I was lifting the flat one into her trunk when it slipped, leaving a black grease mark across the crotch of my khaki pants.

"That was smooth," I muttered. I turned to see her trying unsuccessfully to hide a smile. "I'm going to take a wild guess you don't have a pair of thirty-two, thirty-two dress pants in your car," I said, more as a statement.

She laughed, a deep throaty laugh that made the Raggedy-Ann freckles sprinkled across her cheeks more pronounced.

"I'll take that as a 'no,'" I said.

I started to wipe my hands on my pants, stopped, and after figuring they were ruined anyway, wiped them front and back several times.

"Of course, now I'm going to be late which means I have to work through my lunch," I said, looking down as I wiped my hands again. "And that sucks because I was going to let you buy me lunch as a way of thanking me.

"You can't ask me out any better than that?" she asked, raising an eyebrow.

"I think I was talking about you asking me out, not the other way around."

She studied me for a few moments. "I'm a chef at La Fountain Bleu downtown," she said. She walked to the front driver's side door, opened it, and pulled a business card from her purse. "Give this to the maitre de, and you and your girlfriend will get a free dinner."

"Ouch," I said. "I don't think you can get any more obvious than that. My real question is why you said I should ask you out better, then you invite me to a romantic dinner with my girlfriend."

"So you do have a girlfriend."

We made eye contact, and I bit my lip. "That was a test, wasn't it?"

She nodded. "And I failed miserably," I said.

She nodded again. "Miserably."

"So asking you out now would be a big waste of time."

"I didn't say that."

We stared back and forth. "So how would your boyfriend feel about a strange, good-looking guy changing your tire, admitting he has a girlfriend, and then asking you out anyway?"

"Is this your way of asking if I have a boyfriend?" she asked.

"A girl like you is born with a boyfriend. I'm just trying to figure out if you're a fanatic about it."

She laughed. "You're about as subtle as a train wreck."

"I've always believed that being subtle is incredibly over-rated."

We traded smiles and she finally sighed. "If you have to work through your lunch today, maybe we can have lunch tomorrow."

"Yeah?"

"I don't work on Friday so if you want I'll pick you up where you work tomorrow afternoon."

I clicked my teeth together a few times. "I work for my girlfriend's step-father."

She threw back her head and laughed. "You really are a bastard."

"I was about to ask if you wanted to meet somewhere, but I'm guessing that's a deal-breaker."

"I'll meet you," she said, looking at me over hooded eyelashes. "Say, the Chili's off Turkeyfoot Road at 12:30?"

"My girlfriend works at Chili's," I said. Seeing her reaction, I laughed. "That was a joke. I'll see you tomorrow at 12:30."

She leaned over and gave me a quick kiss on the cheek. "Thanks for changing my tire," she said.

I walked to her driver's side door and opened it. She touched my hand as she got in, and I didn't walk back to my car until her taillights disappeared.

"Unbelievable," I said to no one in particular. I called work to let them know I was going to be late while I changed my pants. The best part of the factory was that no one cared what time I got in as long as I called to let them know I was still alive.

"You look like you had a good morning," said Tonya when I passed her on the way to my desk.

"Huh?"

"Usually, if someone breaks down and then ruins a nice pair of pants, they're not smiling like it's the first day of spring."

"Was I smiling?" I asked, and she nodded. "Maybe because I get to work beside such a beautiful woman each day."

She gave me a cynical eye roll, but that didn't stop the corners of her mouth from turning up. "You're shameless."

The next day, I left at 12:15 for Chili's and got there at almost 12:30 on the dot. Lauren was standing just inside the entrance. The day before she had dressed in black pants and a shapeless white buttoned-down shirt, but wearing a low-cut blouse and skirt, she had an incredible body to go with the beautiful face.

"You are way out of my league," I said, giving her a peck on the cheek.

She looked me up and down. "Are you the guy who helped me yesterday?"

I patted the front of my shirt with both hands. "I look different?"

She shrugged, non-committal. "Is it the angle?" I asked, giving her a glimpse of my profile. "Some people say I look better from the side."

"Maybe it's the lighting," she said after checking me out again.

"Wow," I said when she smiled. "That's what I get for saying something nice. You want the truth? That little piece of fabric that's supposed to pass for a top is too indecent to be worn in public, and that tight skirt showing those legs that seem to go on forever makes you look like a hooker. Granted, I'd have to pay you at least a thousand dollars an hour, but that doesn't change the fact that the people here probably think you're a whore."

She threw back her head and laughed. "Now that sounds like the guy I met yesterday," she said, and then paused, "and that might have been the nicest thing anyone's ever said about me."

She took my hand when the hostess seated us, and I played the role of gentleman, waiting for her to sit down before taking a seat myself. Ironically enough, the same girl who had waited on MaryAnn and I was our waitress. She smiled in recognition when we made eye contact, and my date noticed.

"What was that about?" Lauren asked after the waitress took our drink order and walked away.

"Unlike you, she must think I look pretty good," I said, touching the top and sides of my head, modeling my haircut. "There's not a waitress in the world that can resist the natural."

"You really are full of yourself," she said, shaking her head. "You might have more confidence than any guy I've ever met."

"See, that's what I mean. Girls are always telling guys that confidence is sexy, but the moment he shows any, they try to shoot him out of the saddle."

"There's a difference between confidence and cockiness."

The waitress brought our drinks, and Lauren asked for a few minutes before we made our order.

"You know I'm a chef," she said, looking at the menu. "What exactly do you do?"

"It's actually pretty interesting. I work as a security guard at the mall."

She looked up. "Can't you be serious for five minutes?"

"What makes you think I'm not serious?"

"Hmm, let's see. You're not wearing a uniform, and if you kept your uniform at work, you wouldn't have needed to go home and change your pants yesterday."

"Maybe I'm trying to bring a little class to the position," I said defensively. After a few seconds of not getting a response, I shrugged. "Fine, I'm not a security guard. After hearing what I do, though, you'll understand why I lied about it. I get purchases orders from clients and plug them into a spreadsheet. Sometimes, I have to do basic algebra to calculate price versus product, and on really exciting days I'll get to create spreadsheets using more complicated Excel functions, but the majority of my job consists of mindlessly typing numbers into a spreadsheet."

She rolled her eyes. "That's like saying all I do is take ingredients, throw them in a pan, and then make sure it doesn't burn."

"How about we stop pretending this is a job interview? My idea is that I ask you a question and you have to be completely honest, then you ask me."

"You don't think that's a little Junior High?" she asked, raising an eyebrow.

"Hey, if you're not comfortable giving honest, open answers to sincere questions then we can stare back and forth, maybe talk about the weather if the silence gets too awkward, pretend to be really interested in our food, then leave and never see each other again. Yeah, let's do that. I'm psyched."

"And you'll tell me the absolute truth with trying to throw in stupid jokes?"

"My jokes aren't stupid, thank you very much, but I promise," I said, raising my right hand. "And the rule is that once a question is asked, the other person can't ask the same question."

"So now this Junior High game has rules?"

"Hey, if you'd rather talk about the weather, that's fine with me."

She considered for a moment. "I get to ask the first question?"

"And I'll be completely honest."

"And I can stop the game at any time?"

I shrugged. "Sure."

"Okay," she said, and then thought for a second. "What's the most annoying thing that's ever happened to you on a first date?"

"That's an easy one," I said. "This was maybe five years ago. I met this chick at Starbucks. I'd seen her a couple times, but only to nod and smile. No conversation, really, but she seemed sweet, and she was kind of cute, maybe on the chunky side. One day I'm standing in line and I talk to her for however long it took the barista to make my mocha, and I ask her out to dinner."

"Do you do that a lot?" she interrupted.

"You mean ask girls out?"

She nodded. "No, actually," I said. "Do you want to hear this or not?"

"Only if you want to tell it."

I gave her a bemused frown. "Anyway, we meet at this restaurant, nice place, not black tie or anything, but nice. We start talking, and the conversation goes nowhere. If there's such a thing as less than no personality, this girl had it. So I'm sitting there, telling jokes to lighten the mood, and she's across the table looking at me like I'm reading the obits out of the newspaper."

"What kind of jokes were you telling?"

"What kind of jokes?" I asked, looking at her crossways, and she nodded. "I don't remember, just jokes. What difference does it make?"

"Maybe they were stupid jokes."

I glared at her for a few seconds before continuing. "So she's not reacting at all. Finally, I gave up on conversation, and at that point I'm counting down the minutes until I can get out of there. Anyway, we get our food; I'm wolfing it down, trying to eat as fast as possible, right?"

She nodded, smiling. "She's there, picking at her food, not really eating anything, more pushing it around her plate. Finally, the waiter comes and asks about our food, and if we need anything. I have a mouthful, and I'm in the process of swallowing so I can tell him it's great. Before I can get it out, this girl kind of shields the food with her hand and says, 'can I get a box for this? Maybe my dog will eat it.'"

'Come on," she said.

"I'm serious. The poor waiter, you can tell he doesn't know how to react. After a few seconds, he asks if there's something wrong with her food and she starts ticking them off on her fingers. The lettuce in the salad was too limp, her steak was undercooked, her baked potato was overcooked; saying it so loud, I wanted to put the napkin over my head and crawl out of the place on my hands and knees."

"What did he say?"

"That's the funny part. He offers to take it off the bill, and while he's standing there I ask her who's paying for dinner. She got really offended, and asked if she was supposed to. I said that if I was paying why was she worried about it."

Lauren started laughing. "It gets better," I said. "The waiter, he starts laughing, trying not to show it, but not trying very hard. The people at the table next to us, they're laughing, too. This girl, she calls me about five four-letter words on her way out the door."

"That's pretty bad," Lauren said.

"Needless to say, any time she saw me after that, I got a dirty look. True story."

"Okay, your turn."

I considered for a moment. "If you could do anything, I mean either work-related, where you live, anything, but just one thing, what would you do?"

"You mean that if I get one wish, what would it be?"

"No, because if I said one wish then you could say you wanted more wishes. And it has to be realistic. It can't be world peace, or stopping global warming, or more rainbows and ice cream."

"Anything," she said, exhaling. "Okay. Well, I love my job, so it wouldn't be that," she said and paused. "I like where I live, so it wouldn't be that," pausing again. "Maybe spend a month in Paris? See it with someone who spoke the language and knew where everything was?"

"I think now would be the perfect time to let you know that I'm learning French."

"Be serious," she said, rolling her eyes.

"I've been taking classes for the last six months, and by this time next year I'll probably be speaking it like I've lived there my entire life."

She laughed. "You're an idiot."

"True story."

The waitress walked up just as Lauren was calling me an idiot. "Are you guys ready to order?" she asked, giving me an inquisitive expression that had nothing to do with the menu.

"Go ahead," I said to Lauren.

She looked over the menu. "Hamburger, well-done, no mayo, no cheese, and substitute steamed vegetables for the fries."

"Hopefully this isn't offensive," I said to Lauren, and then to the waitress, "Cheeseburger, extra pepper jack cheese, extra mayo, fries, and a side of ranch dressing."

The waitress smiled and walked away. "There's something going on between you two," Lauren said.

"You mean you don't believe it's the natural?"

She crossed her arms and tucked her chin. "You don't have to tell me if you don't want."

"Okay, but for the record I'm a little insulted you don't think it's simply because I'm such a good-looking guy," I said. "I was in here about a month ago with an ex-girlfriend and she overheard me being a sarcastic jerk. My ex- is really pretty, and she threw a fit when I told

The Amateur

the waitress she was a jealous ex-girlfriend and asked for separate checks."

Lauren laughed. "Okay, my question. If you could re-live one day in your life, what would it be, and why?"

I looked her over. "You're really good at this," I said. "This one is easy, too. This happened around a year ago, February 13. You're going to think I'm lying, but this is the honest to God's truth. The same ex-girlfriend I was in here with a few weeks ago, we'd been going out for a couple years, and I decided to propose. I take her to where we had our first date, and instead of dropping to a knee, I pretended like I was breaking it off."

"Yeah, not my best move," I said, seeing her smile. "Anyway, I'm about to say I want her to marry me when she called me a smug bastard and said she'd been cheating on me. Instead of kicking her to the curb like I would if I had it to do over, I went out, had a one-nighter with some kid's grandmother, and then took her back."

"That's disgusting."

"Definitely not my proudest hour. Okay, my next question is a good one, and remember you have to be honest."

She nodded. "You've been dating a guy for a year," I said, leaning forward. "You're in love and completely happy. What would you do if you came home one day and caught him reading your diary?"

"I don't keep a diary."

"Come on," I said, exasperated. "I told you this is hypothetical. Pretend you do."

"Well, it would depend on if I was seeing another guy, and how honest I was with what I wrote."

I shook my head. "That's not the point. Obviously, he doesn't trust you which is why he's reading it."

"Do you keep a diary?"

"Do I keep a diary? What does that have to do with anything?"

She shrugged. "Just a question."

"So you wouldn't have a problem with it?"

"Why should I have a problem? I'd already know he was insecure, and you said I loved him anyway. I'd just learn to hide it better."

"I don't think that was a real response, so I should get another question."

"It's not my fault it was a stupid question. My turn. What do you like most and least about your family?"

I scratched my head. "I don't know if there's anything I dislike about my family. Sometimes they go out of their way to embarrass me, but I find it kind of endearing. Maybe the way they dress, if I had to pick something, but even that's more funny than it is embarrassing. As for best, I'd definitely say my brother. He's... man, he's a trip. Probably the funniest guy I know, especially when he's not trying to be. The guy, he hates dogs, but he bought a dog to meet a girl he'd never met."

She laughed. "That can't be true."

"Not the best part. They're engaged, I swear to God. He's got the dumbest, funniest one-liners I've ever heard. Every time we get together, we rag on each other non-stop, but any time I get in trouble, he's the one I call."

"That's sweet," she said, reaching across the table to touch my hand.

"Okay, what's the dumbest thing you've ever done?" I asked.

She leaned back. "Dumbest thing," she said, and then paused for a few seconds. "During summer break between my junior and senior year of high school, me and three of my friends went to Cancun for two weeks. We stayed at this really nice resort which cost us around eight-hundred dollars each, which at the time was a lot of money, at least to me. So we'd been there two days when we meet these Mexican guys at the swimming pool at our hotel. They were staying at the resort, so we thought, you know, they were harmless. They said there was a big beach party about a hundred yards from our hotel, and asked us to come. I told my friends it was a bad idea, but since there were a lot of people going, and it was so close to where we were staying they talked me into it. Anyway, we're on the beach, drinking Mexican beer, dancing, feeling pretty good when they start passing out this joint that was as big as my thumb.

She held up her thumb to give the visual effect. "I'd smoked weed a couple times before and never had any problems so I figured, no big deal. Anyway, I took three hits before I realized I wasn't just smoking weed. I remember weaving back to my room, getting sick every few steps, and I vaguely remember falling down in the lobby and my friends carrying me to bed. I was so high I forgot how to breathe. I didn't feel normal until the day before we flew home. So I basically spent the fifteen-hundred dollars I'd saved the previous summer laying in a hotel bed."

Right then, our food arrived. "I'm going to warn you this won't be pretty," I said, putting the napkin in my lap.

She watched me take a few bites, and then shook her head. "Save any comments until after we eat," she said.

"Is that a knock on my eating habits?" I asked through a mouthful of food.

That generated an amused expression. "I can't imagine why any girl would have lunch with you twice."

"So asking you to meet me for lunch tomorrow is out of the question?" I asked through the same mouthful of food."

"Shut up and eat."

I kept sneaking glances at her throughout my meal, and I'd catch her watching me, a little smile touching the corners of her mouth. "I can't wait to see you eat a meal I cook, see if you give it the business like you're doing with that cheeseburger," she said.

We finished eating and after her making a swipe for the check I grabbed it and stuck in two twenties. "You can pay next time," I said.

"I guess you need to get back to work?"

I took the cell phone from my pocket. "If I take a half-day, you want to go for a walk?"

She shrugged. "Sure, why not?"

Chapter 14

I called Tonya and said I would be out the rest of the day. She didn't even ask why.

"Presidents Park is right down the street," I said to Lauren. "You driving or me?"

She pointed to herself and we travelled the three or four miles to the park. The parking lot was practically empty, and we parked at the far end next to a shelter. The sun was occasionally peaking through the clouds, but the wind made it feel ten degrees cooler. There was a path that began a few steps from where Lauren's car was parked, and we started walking, probably a little closer together than if it had been summertime.

"I think it's still my turn," she said. "Name your worst high school moment."

"God, this is bringing back horrible memories," I said, cringing. "I'll tell you, but you have to swear not to call me by my high school nickname, and you can never repeat this story to another human being."

"Wow! This is going to be good."

I took a deep breath. "My freshman year, I accidentally set the school on fire."

She laughed. "On fire?"

"The way it happened, me and another guy were standing in front of my locker playing with a cigarette lighter. My older brother had shown me how you could shoot the flame really high if you took off the top and adjusted the cog wheel. You know what the cog wheel is?"

"Sure, the thingy under the metal part."

"Right. So we were huddled together so that no one else could see, and I did my little magic trick. In those days, I always carried a bottle of hair spray in my coat, and I guess some of it soaked through."

"Hair spray? Were you a fourteen-year old girl?"

"You know, this is tough enough talking about without you making fun of me."

"Do you still wear hairspray?"

"Sometimes a little gel," I said, exasperated. "Can I get back to the story, please?"

"I can hardly wait."

I paused. "Where was I?"

"Hairspray in your coat."

"Thank you," I said. "So the hairspray had soaked through my coat, right? Well, the moment the flame hit the coat it became a huge fireball. Not thinking, I tried to smother the flame with what was left of my coat, but all that did was cause the books and papers in my locker to catch fire, too. I threw my coat into the hallway, and about ten seconds later the sprinklers came on, flooding the entire area. Luckily, the school didn't kick me out, but I was suspended for a week. Upon my return, I was immortalized as "the Fire Guy."

"The fire guy?" she asked, closing her eyes, she was laughing so hard.

"Remember you swore never to repeat it."

She tilted her head like she was considering. "Okay, but if I don't, I get to ask the next question."

"You really are a cheater," I muttered.

"If I wasn't I wouldn't be here, and neither would you."

I laughed. "Point taken."

"You've been married for two years and come home to find your wife in bed with her best friend," she said. "What would you do?"

"Is her best friend male or female?"

"Female."

"Is she hot? Like, give me a scale, one to ten."

"I don't know," she said, rolling her eyes. "Seven."

"Wait," I said, coming to a stop. "Are you asking because you're bisexual?"

"Be serious."

"Because you're at least a ten," I said, walking again. "At the very least."

"Are you going to answer the question or not?"

I thought about it. "Honestly, I'd probably act like it didn't bother me, but I'd have a hard time trusting her after that. If she didn't tell me about her best friend, then she's probably messing around with guys, too. That said, if they asked me to participate, I probably would."

"You're a pig."

"You wanted honesty, I gave you honesty. My question: What's the best pickup line a guy has used on you?"

"Other than your line, 'so call them back,'" she asked, mimicking me.

"Hey, it worked, didn't it?"

"Best pickup line," she repeated. "Okay, I was at a bar with a few of my friends when a guy comes over with a deck of cards and asks if we want to see a magic trick. We say 'yes' and he asks me to pick a card. I choose one and he turns his head while I put it back in the deck, then he shuffles them a few times and pulls out the card."

I rolled my eyes. "It's a trick deck. You can pick one up almost anywhere."

"That's what I said, but he told me he was a real magician and could prove it by guessing my phone number. I say there's no way he could do that, and he says, 'you're probably right. Why don't you go ahead and write it down.'"

I laughed. "That's awesome. Did you give him your number?"

"Of course not."

"Then how can that be better than 'so call them back?'"

"You didn't say it in a bar. What's your best pickup line ever?"

"That question is illegal because it's a repeat of my question."

"That's ridiculous."

"The rules of the game were established before it started."

She shook her head, acting like she wasn't amused. "Okay, fine," I said, taking a deep breath and blowing it out slow. "Before I start, I want to make it clear that I've only had two one-nighters in my life, swear to God."

"Then I'm guessing it worked."

"You are never going to respect me again after I tell you this one," I said. "Me and a buddy of mine were in Atlanta, this is maybe five years ago. We're shooting pool at this college bar and there's a girl I've been flirting with all night."

"What do you mean by all night?"

"Like, two or three hours. Anyway, I'm in the middle of a game when she announces she's leaving. She takes maybe two steps, and I call out, asking where she lives. She looks at me like I'm crazy and asks why I want to know. I tell her I need to tell my buddy where to pick me up in the morning."

"What did she say?" she asked, laughing.

I shrugged. "She gave me directions, and my buddy picked me up the next day."

"Tell me the truth," she said, coming to a stop. I turned and she looked into my eyes. "Do you try to seduce every woman you meet or am I special?"

"Wait a second. First, that's two questions, and second, it's my turn."

"You're taking this game way too seriously."

"So you want to stop," I said, shrugging my shoulders. "Okay, that was our deal. You get to ask the first and last question which doesn't seem fair, but I'll play by the rules."

"We can still play question and answer if it makes you happy, but I was thinking something more adult, like having an every day, normal conversation. If the other makes you feel better, though, ask your question."

"You make me sound like an insolent child," I pouted. "Can I ask more question if I answer the one about seducing women?"

"I don't have any reason to lie, so why should that matter?"

"I got a good answer for that," I said quickly. "Sometimes I ask really stupid questions, but in the framework of the game you have to answer."

"You might be the most idiotic, profoundly interesting guy I've ever met."

I studied her. "I'm trying to figure out how to take that one."

"It's definitely a compliment."

"I'll take it. Do I try to seduce every woman I meet," I said, more to myself. "I don't think so, and at the beginning I wasn't trying to seduce you. In fact, I'm not trying to seduce you now, not really anyway. With me, I try to charm beautiful women, even not so beautiful women. I like to make people laugh."

I thought about it. "Honestly, I just try to be funny all the time. I'm not sure why, really. I guess I've been doing it so long, it's second nature. Maybe so people won't take me too seriously? Maybe so they'll like me?"

I shrugged. "No idea, but in answer to your question, no, I don't try to seduce every woman I meet. Can I ask my question now?"

"Go ahead," she said, rolling her eyes.

"We've been talking for over a half hour now. What do you like most and least about this date?"

She hesitated. "I don't think there's anything I don't like."

The path went down and around, and trees canopied overhead. Even though there were no leaves, the limbs blocked out the majority of the sky. We kept walking, her looking at the ground, and me with hands in pockets. I was surprised when I opened my cell phone and saw it was after five.

"I need to get home," I said, apologetic.

We drove back to my car, and she pulled up into the parking spot next to where my car was sitting.

"I hope I can see you again," she said.

I looked at her for a long moment. "What are you doing tonight?"

She smiled. "Cooking you dinner."

She wrote her address and phone number on a small scrap of paper, and gave me a peck on the cheek before she drove away. I checked my cell as I was getting in the car, and sure enough I had five missed calls, all from Amber. Without listening to any of them, I called her back.

"Hey," I said when she answered, "I would have called earlier, but I thought you were probably sleeping, and I accidentally turned off my cell. Is everything okay?"

"My step-father told me you took a half-day," she said, sounding concerned.

I cleared my throat. "Yeah, I had a migraine so I just walked around trying to make it go away."

"Do you want me to call in?"

This wasn't going very well. That's what happens when you're a bad liar and get put on the spot. "I'm okay now. I'll probably just take a few Advil and take a nap."

There was a brief silence. "Okay," she said. "I made dinner and it's in the fridge. All you need to do is heat it up."

By the time I got to the apartment, she was already gone. I got a quick shower and changed into a nice pair of slacks and a buttoned-down shirt. I was on my way out the door when I remembered dinner. Amber had made a ham and cheese casserole, and I cut out a generous chunk, then got a small plastic grocery bag from a kitchen cabinet and put in the food. Thinking about it a little more, I set the bag on the kitchen table and grabbed a pair of sweatpants, a sweatshirt, and a pair of tennis shoes. I balanced it all and slowly walked to my car.

The plastic bag was deposited into a convenience store dumpster, and I arrived at Lauren's place at a little before six. It was a really nice apartment building, very stylish, and she lived on the ground floor.

"You should have called," she said breathlessly when she opened the door.

"My girlfriend is fanatical about my cell phone records," I said after she ushered me in. Lauren laughed when she noticed the outfit I was carrying.

"There's a glass of white wine on the counter," she said, giving me a quick peck on the cheek before walking back into the kitchen. "Appetizers will be ready in two minutes."

"I can safely say that no woman has ever cooked me a meal that included appetizers," I said, looking around.

Her apartment was incredible. She had what had to be at least a sixty-inch television mounted on the wall, fully-stocked bar sitting next to it, a huge overstuffed couch, and two E-Z chairs.

"The only thing keeping this place from being the perfect bachelor pad is a stripper pole in the middle of the living room," I said, raising my voice.

She walked into the dining room carrying a dish with six pieces of something covered with bacon. I was about fifteen feet away when I caught the smell, and it set my mouth to watering.

"How am I supposed to eat these?" I asked, grabbing one of the appetizers off the plate and popping it in my mouth.

"Not like that," she said, laughing.

"This is really good," I said, hiding my mouth.

She shook her head. "Where you raised by wolves?"

"How would I know these were scallops instead of fish if I was raised by wolves?" I asked, chasing down the appetizer with a long swallow of wine.

"Your parents must be very proud."

We stared back and forth throughout the appetizers, neither of us saying more than the occasional stray word. She made filet mignon for the entrée and paired it with a bottle of cabernet.

"I don't want to play your game again, but why did you stop and help me yesterday?" she asked.

I thought about it. "Honestly, I'm not really sure," I said. "I didn't see you until I walked back, and I definitely don't do that sort of thing on a regular basis. The only thing I can come up with is that maybe I associate those new VW bugs with hot girls. As far as asking you out, though, I don't know. I think I knew I was going to ask after I took about three steps from my car. Not part of the game, but I have a follow-up question. Why did you call the person who was coming to get you when I offered to help?"

"Beyond the obvious reason that I didn't feel like waiting beside the road for half an hour and being late for work, I thought you were cute," she said, and then paused. "And you made me laugh."

Her expression turned got serious. "There aren't many guys out there who can do that. When you stopped to help me, and you started walking toward my car, I still didn't think I'd go out with you, not in a million years."

I started to say 'okay' when she continued. "But you were really sweet," she said, and looked down at the table for a few seconds before looking into my eyes.

"Sweet like chocolate, or sweet like an old lady pushing a shopping cart?" I asked.

"Neither one," she said, laughing. "You really are a dork."

"So why did you agree to go out with me even though you know I have a girlfriend?"

"Because I have a boyfriend, and it's a lot easier to date someone who's in a relationship."

"That makes sense."

She stopped. "But it's not like I'm out pursuing a relationship or anything like that. In fact, I haven't gone out with anyone since I've been with my boyfriend."

"Okay. It's not a big deal."

"I know people always say that a woman knows she's going to cheat before she leaves her house, but making you dinner was the furthest thing from my mind when you asked me out."

I held up a hand. "Look, I get it, okay? You didn't expect anything to happen, but that's the thing about chemistry. You either connect with someone or you don't. If you connect with someone, you shouldn't have to explain it."

She made some kind of sorbet for dessert, and after a few bites she asked if I wanted to sit on the couch and watch a movie. We weren't kissing or anything; we just sat there, her head on my shoulder. I don't think I'd felt that kind of chemistry with anyone my entire life. Before I knew it, it was after eleven.

"I have to go," I said.

Her mouth turned down, but then she quickly smiled. "Of course," she said.

I pushed myself off the couch and she walked me to the door. "Thank you," I said, looking into her eyes.

Her arms circled my neck and she pulled me toward her and we kissed. It was almost, but not quite, innocent. After a few seconds, she buried her face against my shoulder.

"I had a lot of fun today," she said in a small voice. I leaned down and kissed her neck, breathing her in. She smelled intoxicating, a mixture of sweat and wine and some kind of subtle, delicate perfume.

"I really have to go," I said.

She turned. "Your clothes," she said, walking to where I'd left them in the living room. I started unbuttoning my shirt and slipped off my shoes.

"I was going to suggest you do that in the bathroom," she said when I was down to my boxers. She touched my chest when I was putting on my sweats and gave me a kiss as I pulled on my sweatshirt. I started to fold the clothes I'd worn, when Lauren stopped me.

"Leave them here and you can pick them up next time," she said.

"Yeah? When's next time?"

"Tomorrow?"

"My girlfriend doesn't have another night shift until next Tuesday."

"Tuesday night?"

I smiled. "I can hardly wait."

I got home a little after midnight and after quickly brushing my teeth and washing my face I was in bed. Less than five minutes after I turned off the lights I heard Amber come through the front door, and a few seconds after that she came into the bedroom. After giving me a quick kiss she walked out into the living room. Once I heard the television go on, I rolled onto my back and stared at the ceiling. The day with Lauren was as good as any I'd ever had. She was beautiful, she was smart, sexy; the only flaw was that she was a cheater, but I could hardly complain about that.

The next morning Amber was quiet over breakfast, and I could tell something was wrong. I could also tell it had nothing to do with me.

"Reliable is asking me to go to Salt Lake City for training," she finally said. I didn't comment, just waited for her to continue. "It's a really great opportunity, but I'll be gone for two weeks."

There was a brief silence. "When would you leave?" I asked.

"Tuesday morning," she said, and then added quickly, "I won't go if you think it's a bad idea."

We'd had the same conversation when she took the new position. "Two weeks isn't that long," I said, circling around the table. I took a seat in the chair beside her, and pulled her against my shoulder. "If I were you, I'd rather have the training in San Diego or somewhere like that, but I'm sure training in the desert around a bunch of people who think drinking will send you straight to hell will be a great experience."

"Then you're okay with it?"

"More than okay," I said, kissing the top of her head.

The weekend was spent getting stuff together, taking her suits to the dry cleaners, and her making sure I knew how to make dinner without burning down the house. Monday, we went to see a movie, and even though I told her not to worry about it she cooked three casseroles, as she put it, "just in case."

Her flight was at 7:00 AM on Tuesday morning, and I dropped her off at the airport around five. It was too early to go to the office, so I went home, planning to close my eyes for a few minutes. The next time I opened them it was after eight.

After a brief inspection in the mirror, I deemed myself presentable, and got to the office about twenty minutes late which was no small feat. No one even noticed. The day dragged on, partly because I was so tired, but also from the anticipation of seeing Lauren in a few hours. From a pure chemistry perspective, it was scary. I remembered thinking I'd never find a girl as beautiful as MaryAnn, but Lauren blew her out of the water.

After I got out of work, I called Lauren to let her know I'd be there around six. It took half an hour to get home, another hour or so to get ready, and about fifteen minutes to talk to Amber so she wouldn't worry. By the time I got to Lauren's place it was ten after six.

"So, elephant in the room, when's your boyfriend coming back to town?" I asked once we were seated at the dining room table.

She shrugged. "This weekend, next weekend, I never really know."

"Meaning he could be on his way over now?"

"He always calls a few days in advance," she said, and then paused. "Of course, he might want to surprise me."

"Your boyfriend, is he a big guy, or…"

She smiled. "Ex-special forces."

"What about foot speed?" I asked, brushing my forehead like I was wiping away perspiration. "Have you ever seen him in a race?"

She threw back her head and laughed. "I'm guessing you're not much of a tough guy."

"My grandmother used to tell me that she'd rather hear people say look at that coward run than doesn't he look natural."

"It sounds like your grandmother was a smart woman."

"I took her advice to heart," I said. "I've only lost one fight in my life, and that was the time I tripped over the curb when I was rounding a street corner."

"You really are a one-of-a-kind guy," she said, and thought about it. "You're more like a woman."

"That's quite a jump," I said, leaning back in my chair.

"I mean that in a good way."

"More like a woman," I muttered. "If my brother heard you say that I'd have to move away and change my name."

"Learn to take a compliment."

"You call that a compliment? Telling me I have pretty eyes or that I have a nice smile is a compliment. Saying I'm like a woman? Definitely not a compliment."

She rolled her eyes. "All you're doing is proving my point when you cry like a girl."

I stood and took three long strides around the table, then grabbed her, lifting her out of the chair. Her body tensed for a second, but that went away when I kissed her. She had the kind of full lips that were made for kissing, and after about thirty seconds, I stepped back so we could each take a breath.

"Kiss me again," she gasped, putting her arms around my waist. We did a sideways stumble toward the couch, but didn't quite make it there. A half hour later we were panting on the carpet, our clothes in a pile a few feet away.

"Definitely not a woman," she said.

"Let me know if you need more convincing later on," I said, propping myself up with an elbow.

She kissed my forehead as she got up and I watched the hypnotic way her hips twitched as she walked into the kitchen. A minute or so later, she came back carrying two glasses of red wine. We sat on the couch and touched and tasted while a movie was playing in the background. About halfway through, we walked back to her bedroom.

Around 9:30, I got out of bed to go to the bathroom. "You have to go," she said, more statement than question.

I laughed. "Bathroom, not front door. My girlfriend will be out of town for the next two weeks," I said, and then paused. "Second thought, I do need to get home because I'm sure she'll call."

That generated a laugh. "You are a tremendous bastard, telling me that you need to go home so you can talk to your girlfriend while you stand naked in my bedroom."

"The thing I was wondering is how your boyfriend would feel if he came in this weekend to find out that another guy had been occupying his side of your bed."

"Touché."

I got home and found Amber had left a message on the machine about twenty minutes earlier asking that I call her back.

"Sorry, I was in the bathroom," I said when she answered.

There was a short pause. "I just wanted to say I miss you. Salt Lake City is a lot better than I expected, but it would be even better if you were here."

"I wish I was there, too," I said, staring at the ceiling.

After less than five minutes, we exchanged "I love you's," and not long after that I was on my way back to Lauren's place. She was right. I was a tremendous bastard.

Chapter 15

The game Lauren and I played was filled with excitement and danger. We got together every chance we could; sometimes three times a week, others, not at all. No matter how often it happened, though, it never got old. And it wasn't just in the bedroom. I could sit and talk to her for hours without struggling for conversation. Despite our connection, it didn't really bother me when her boyfriend was in town. That part didn't make sense, especially to me, but it was true.

Tuesday was typically the night we'd hook up except when she was with her boyfriend. On this particular Tuesday, Amber had the Reliable spring party, which unlike any company I'd heard, didn't allow spouses or significant other non-employees to attend. Lauren's boyfriend was in town, and I had planned on a boring evening at home, so I was surprised when I walked to my car after work and found a note under my windshield wiper with the words "call me" scrawled in Lauren's handwriting. I stopped at a convenience store phone booth, and she answered on the first ring.

"You okay?" I asked.

"Do you want to come over tonight?" she asked, sounding like she'd been crying.

"You'll have to give me at least an hour," I said, and then paused. "I mean, I need that kind of time to make myself presentable and talk to Amber, but if it's an emergency I'll stop by now."

"No emergency," she said. I definitely heard a sniffle. "I'll make dinner. Be here at seven?"

"Seven o'clock. I'll be there."

Amber was already gone when I got home, and after a quick pit stop at the bathroom and washing my hands, I gave her a call.

"Hey, sweetie," she said, slurring the words, "how are you?"

The party had started almost two hours earlier so I figured it had to be the alcohol.

"It sounds like you're feeling pretty good," I said.

She laughed a little too loud. "Getting drunk is the only way these people are even mildly interesting."

"Oh boy," I muttered, and then louder, "sweetie, try to keep your voice down."

"I saw your friend, Steve."

"Goderwis?"

"Is there another one?" she asked. "He tried to hit on me, can you believe it?"

I pinched my nose with my thumb and index finger. "What did you say?"

She laughed a little louder. "I said he was a tool and to go away before I told his wife."

"You know at least one person gets fired each year for stuff they do at that stupid party," I said, eyes closed.

"What was I supposed to do, give him a lap dance? Anyway, I have to go. My drink is down to ice cubes, and I don't know when they'll close the bar."

"You already got a cab voucher, right?"

"Yes, Dad," she said sarcastically.

"Promise if any of the other guys hit on you that you'll just walk away without saying anything."

"You jealous?" she asked with a little attitude.

I rolled my eyes. "Just be careful."

"You are such a buzz kill," she said. The next thing I heard was a dial tone. I took my time getting showered and dressed, and still had an hour to waste. After forty minutes of alternatively watching Sportscenter and the clock, I headed over to Lauren's place.

She opened the door before I had a chance to ring the bell. There was a smile on her face, but her eyes were red.

"There's a bottle of wine on the table," she said.

I stood in the doorway, waiting for her to tell me what was wrong. "He broke up with me," she said after a few seconds.

"You okay?" I asked, scanning her face.

"First he tells me he has to leave town because of a business emergency, and after he was gone less than half an hour, the prick called and said I loved him too much and he needed his space," she said, putting her head on my shoulder. "He didn't even have the balls to tell me in person."

"How could he want his space? You only see him a couple days a month."

"That's what I said. He told me that maybe down the road we could meet up again, but for now he just wanted to be alone. Then he said he left a going away present in my dresser."

She held back her hair so I could see the earrings. The diamonds were huge.

"Are those real?" I asked.

"Don't you know what this means? He knew he was going to break up with me before he left the apartment. Instead of saying it face-to-face, he had to do it over the phone."

I didn't say anything, just rubbed the back of her neck. She didn't really cry, and when she looked up she was more mad than upset.

"How much do you think I can get for the earrings?" she asked.

I laughed. "No idea."

"All the guy did was buy jewelry. He didn't have a creative bone in his body."

"So you're going to sell all the jewelry?"

She considered. "I won't sell it all, just enough to go on a nice vacation to Europe. Send the smug jerk a picture saying wish you were here, and thanks."

"Wow! That must be a lot of jewelry."

She shrugged. "We dated over six months, and he brought jewelry practically every time he came to town."

"You sure it's not costume jewelry?" I asked, only half-kidding.

"I'm not stupid. The first time we met, he gave me this long story about how he was a contractor and made all this money. Before he left, he gave me a diamond and sapphire ring, and told me he'd be back in a few weeks. I got it appraised, and it was worth over five grand. I figure I have somewhere in the neighborhood of a hundred-thousand if I sold it all."

"That should pay for a really nice vacation."

She laughed. "Anyway, I made veal and roast potatoes."

"Nice," I said, following her into the kitchen. She poured us each a glass of red wine, and we sat at the dining room table.

"I'm not asking you to break up with your girlfriend or anything like that. I want to make sure you…"

"Never crossed my mind," I interrupted.

"But I need you to be honest and tell me if you think there's a chance I'll meet a nice guy," she said, and then paused, "somebody who isn't looking at his watch every five minutes thinking about how much time he has before he needs to get home to his girlfriend."

"That was a shot at me, wasn't it?"

She laughed, but then her face turned serious. "So honestly, am I just a fun girl or a relationship girl?"

"You're asking the wrong guy. I'm with, hands-down, the best girl I've ever dated and I've been sneaking out on nights she's working to see you. At least you only see me on days your boyfriend is out of town. I leave your bed and go home to her."

I thought for a second. "That sounds horrible, doesn't it? I definitely don't qualify for giving that kind of advice. I'm not a relationship-guy, that's for sure."

"I thought about that," she said. "At the beginning, definitely not since then, but at the beginning, I was hoping you'd ask me to break up with my boyfriend and that you'd leave your girlfriend, and somehow us two cheaters could be faithful."

I laughed. "I thought about it, too, but I came to the same conclusion. No way we could ever trust each other."

"That doesn't mean it isn't fun," she said quickly.

"Absolutely not," I said.

We were halfway through appetizers when my phone vibrated. I looked down and saw it was Amber. I motioned for Lauren to be quiet.

"Everything okay?" I asked.

There was a pause. "Is this Houston?" a male voice asked.

I stood up and put the napkin on the table. "Who's this?"

"It's Brad," he said, and then, "Campbell. I was on your old team at Reliable."

"What's wrong with Amber?"

"She's okay. I mean, she's not really okay, but she's not hurt or anything. We're outside the convention center and she's laying on the sidewalk asking for you."

"Is she just drunk or is something else wrong, too?"

"I don't know if there's anything else, but she's definitely drunk."

I heard Amber in the background. "Is that Houston?" she asked.

"Here," he said awkwardly after a short pause. I heard something moving in the background, and then the clatter when the phone landed on concrete.

"Houston, where are you?" Amber asked.

Lauren was watching me with an annoyed expression. "I'm having dinner," I said, my eyes on Lauren. "Are you okay?"

"I tried to get a cab, but the driver drove off when I puked on the side of his car," she said, and then in a small voice, "can you come pick me up?"

I hesitated, but only for a split second. "I'll be there in twenty minutes. Will you put Brad on the phone?"

A few seconds later, a tentative, "Hello?"

"Brad, do me a favor. Just take her inside so she doesn't get arrested. I'll be there in a few minutes."

I hung up the phone and looked at Lauren. "Are you kidding me?" she asked.

"I have to go," I said, getting to my feet.

"Do you know how long it took me to put this together? If you care about me at all you'll call someone to pick her up."

"I like you a lot," I said softly, "but you were right about what you said. We just have fun together. Amber's the one I go home to every night."

Tears pinched the corner of her eyes. "If you walk out, don't bother coming back."

I stopped at the door. "I know you won't forgive me, but I'm sorry. I had more fun with you than anyone I've ever met. The guy who ends up with you will get a great girl. You're definitely relationship-material," I said, and then paused. "Just not with me."

It only took twenty minutes to get to the convention center, but I spent another ten trying to find a parking spot. Finally, I just stopped on the street outside of the building and put on my hazard lights. I walked into the convention center, and Amber was sprawled on an aluminum chair surrounded by four people.

I had dressed up for dinner, at least by my standards, but I was still decidedly underdressed. The Reliable spring party always had a prom-like feel, and ball gowns and tuxedos were the outfits of choice. The people surrounding Amber scattered once they recognized me, and a crowd gathered about twenty feet away when word spread that I was in the building. I caught a few head nods, but just as many, if not more, turned away.

"I'm really messed up," she moaned when I started to lift her out of the chair. She had vomit all over her four-hundred dollar dress and I could smell it in hair as well.

"Tony, you mind helping me, buddy?" I asked a guy I recognized who was standing to my right. We carried her, feet barely touching the ground, out to the passenger side of my Corolla. The crowd followed us outside and once she was strapped into the passenger side I circled around. I fought the urge to give all of them the finger as we drove away.

"You okay?" I asked after we'd gone a mile or two.

She had her face pressed against the glass, and her eyes were closed. She mumbled unintelligibly and I patted her leg.

"Let me know if you need to throw up," I said.

I'm not sure what she said, but it came out more like a musical hum. We made it home and I carried her up the stairs. By the time we got to the door, my back was hurting.

"You look nice," she slurred as I laid her on the living room couch.

"I think that might be the alcohol talking."

I could see her trying to focus on my shirt, but her pupils were pinpoints. "Did you dress up just to come get me?"

"Something like that. You want some water?"

She considered for a moment before nodding. "Lots of ice," she called out as I walked into the kitchen.

I filled a thirty-two ounce cup with water from the tap, but by the time I got to her she had passed out. Her feet were still on the floor, but her body was twisted so that she was lying on her side, face on the couch cushion. The dress was hiked up to just above her knees. I pulled her legs onto the couch and took off her shoes. She opened her eyes briefly and smiled, then just as quickly went back to sleep. There was still some vomit at the corners of her mouth so I went to the bathroom and got a cold rag. She flinched when I started wiping her mouth, but then smiled, eyes still closed.

"You really are a great boyfriend," she said.

"I don't know about all that."

"Do you have any idea how many people at the party came up to me and said I was way too good for you?"

I laughed. "No clue."

"At least twenty, and most of them were guys."

"Not a big surprise."

"Some guy tried to kiss me, and I bit his lip."

I stopped. "Who?"

"I bit it so hard I think I made it bleed," she said, and laughed.

"Who was it?"

Her forehead wrinkled like she was thinking. "He was kind of short and had bad breath."

"Drink this, it'll make you feel better," I said, holding the cup to her lips. "You want some pretzels or anything?"

She took a loud slurp, and shook her head. "Did I tell you that Steve hit on me?"

"You mentioned it."

"No, he did it again."

I rubbed my forehead with the hand not holding the cup. "What did you say?"

"I told him that I could stand and talk to him all night, but I remembered I had two legs and he was a dumbass."

"You didn't talk like that to anyone else, did you?"

"Only the assholes who said you were a jerk," she said defensively.

"Thanks for sticking up for me," I said, sitting adjacent to her in the recliner. "Get some rest."

I put the odds at about seven to five that she wouldn't have a job by the end of the week. That carried over to me thinking about how good I had things. I'd told Lauren the truth. Once the fun was over, I always went home to Amber.

I took off my shirt and after briefly considering putting it in the laundry basket I threw it in the trash.

"I'm going to be sick," Amber said, running past me to the bathroom.

She didn't quite make it. The hardwood floor was definitely going to need a good scrubbing. She was bent over the toilet when I got there with the cup of water. Her hair was matted to the porcelain and I pulled it away as she took another drink. I got another rag from the closet and ran it under cold water before wiping her face and putting it on the back of her neck.

"You need anything else?" I asked, starting to get up.

She grabbed my wrist. "Will you hold me?" she asked in a small voice.

I got down on my knees and she rested her head against my chest. "You love me, don't you," she said, looking up.

I touched her face affectionately. "You know I do."

"That makes it all okay," she said, smiling as she closed her eyes. "I'm sure you've been with other girls since we've been together, but I know you love me the most."

"Amber, don't say that," I said, putting my forehead against hers.

"It's true. You treat me better than any guy I've ever known." She paused. "Did I ever tell you about my father, my real father?"

I started to say "yes," but she continued. "He's an alcoholic, and he never really cared about me at all. And then there's Tom," she said, coughing out a laugh. "He's always telling me to call him Dad and he's always saying how much he loves me, but I know good and well if him and my mom ever split up I'd never see him again. You're the only guy I know who'd never leave."

"I'm not going anywhere," I said, kissing the top of her head.

"So that makes it all okay. Just promise you won't leave me."

"I swear."

You'd think that getting permission to mess around would make me feel better considering the circumstances, but it actually made me feel worse. This was a girl who counted on me, needed me, a girl who wouldn't cheat on me no matter what, and I messed around at every opportunity, which didn't make any sense. The old phrase is that cheater's cheat, but I had never cheated on any other girl I'd dated, at least not unless sleeping with that old woman classified as cheating. And Amber was head and shoulders over MaryAnn with the exception of physical attraction, and even that was debatable.

"I love you," she said, her voice muffled by my chest.

"I love you, too."

She looked up. "I know you have to work in the morning so you can go back to bed," she said, even though her eyes said otherwise. "I'll be okay."

I touched her forehead. "I can stay up for a while. Drink this even if it makes your stomach hurt."

She took the cup and after a few timid swallows, she tipped back the cup and took a long gulp. Sure enough, no sooner had she done so it came back up.

"Drink a little at a time," I said, holding her hair back.

Her eyes were watering. "Leave me alone," she groaned.

I put more cold water on the washcloth and added some ice from the cup. She initially resisted when I put her head in my lap, but once I started rubbing the back of her neck she closed her eyes and fell asleep.

I kept rubbing her head, and the next thing I knew, I was laying with my shoulders against the wall. Amber murmured when I picked her up, but barely moved when I carried her to bed. Once I laid her face down, I pulled off her dress and hung it on the door. More than likely, it was ruined based on the stains that went from top to bottom.

The next morning, I opened my eyes and looked over at the clock. It was a little after eight. Amber was next to me, face down, and had shrugged off the blanket to the point that just a small portion of her back was covered. It took a few seconds to remember the day of the week. Wednesday. Amber worked eight-thirty to five on Wednesday.

"Sweetie, wake up," I said, shaking her. She didn't twitch. "It's after eight," I said, raising my voice.

Her head popped up, eyes wide. "No," she moaned, almost crying. "I can't be late today."

Reliable had a strict policy about calling in sick or late the day after the party. It was basically that you had to be in the hospital or dead. Coming in hung over was okay, but your butt better be in your seat once your shift started.

She wrinkled her nose. "I smell like puke," she complained when she started putting on her clothes.

"Get dressed, and I'll think of something," I said. I walked into the bathroom while she was putting on her clothes and put her toothbrush and a tube of toothpaste in a zip-lock bag.

"I can't believe I drank so much," she said.

"You're going to catch hell today, and drinking doesn't have anything to do with it."

"God, don't remind me."

"Call me before you get out so I can pick you up."

She was putting on her shoes, but stopped. "My car's at the convention center," she said.

I laughed. "I was going to drop you off and pick you up anyway."

"I'm a lucky girl," she said, an affectionate smile on her face.

I left that one alone. We were in the car by 8:20, and I covered the five miles from our apartment to her building in record time.

"You want me to call from the hospital and say there's a family emergency?" I asked as I pulled up to the entrance.

She snorted. "It's not like there's anyone here I need to impress."

"If you change your mind, call my cell," I said as she opened the passenger side door. She leaned back in and gave me a kiss.

"I love you," she said over her shoulder as she hurried toward the door.

After I dropped her off, I called the florist and ordered a dozen long-stem roses and had them sent to Amber with a little note attached that read, "no matter what happens today, remember there's a guy at home who isn't going anywhere." The kind of day that she was about to have, she needed as much sunshine as possible. The next thing I did was call a separate florist across town and ordered a dozen for Lauren. The only note I added said, "Goodbye and good luck. I'm sorry."

The fact that I wanted to spend the rest of my life with Amber wasn't going to make me miss Lauren any less.

Chapter 16

The longer I worked at the factory, the more Tonya and I flirted back and forth. For me, it was basically just as a way to pass the time. As time went on, though, I found myself oddly attracted to her; odd because she was clearly not my type. She was attractive in a trashy kind of way, and once in a while I would find myself fantasizing about how crazy she was in bed. The biggest problem I had with that fantasy was the dead tooth. And she had two kids. And, of course, she was married. I'd done a lot of morally questionable things in my life, but I'd never messed around with a married woman.

The weekend before Amber's birthday, I went to the mall to pick up a gift. I was on my way out to the parking lot when I saw MaryAnn coming through the entrance accompanied by a tall guy who looked vaguely familiar.

She looked at me and sniffed a little as she stuck her nose in the air. "Hello," she said, saying it like I was a Jehovah's Witness knocking on her door.

"MaryAnn," I said, giving her my best smile, "I don't know if you remember me or not."

I stuck out my hand to the guy who was with her. "Houston," I said. "MaryAnn and I were engaged once upon a time."

"You were right," he said to MaryAnn, still looking at me. "He definitely thinks he's funny."

"Come on," I said. "That wasn't just a little funny?"

"We're in a hurry," MaryAnn snapped, grabbing his arm.

"Wait a second," I said. "I know you from somewhere."

He was still smiling. "I work at the same school as MaryAnn."

"That's it," I said, nodding. "You're the gym teacher, right?"

Still smiling. "I'm surprised you remember."

I took a step back and looked him over. "Last time I saw you, you were wearing a towel. I definitely like the jeans and t-shirt combo more."

That got a laugh. "What do you think, MaryAnn?" he asked. "I look better with this or the towel?"

"Josh, we need to go or we'll be late for the movie," she said.

As much as I didn't want to, I liked the guy. "Seriously, though, I know you from somewhere else," I said.

We looked back and forth. "I know," he said, eyes narrowing. "You're the guy who was screwing my girlfriend behind my back. I've been looking for you."

I tried to pout, but couldn't hide the smile. "Right when I thought we would be friends you say something like that."

"I can't blame you, though," I said, giving MaryAnn a sly grin. "She's a fire-cracker."

"Josh," MaryAnn said, more as a question.

"I'd have been a lot more pissed off about it if she hadn't been seeing all those other guys, too."

"You're so immature," MaryAnn said.

The light bulb went off. "Town and Country," I said. "I played against you in a basketball league there."

He looked at me for a long moment and shook his head. "Drawing a blank."

"I dropped somewhere in the neighborhood of thirty points on you. Maybe if you were looking up at me from under the basket with my foot on your chest I'd look more familiar."

He looked at me with an inquisitive expression for a few seconds. "You're that guy," he said, the recognition registering. "You kept running your mouth every time up and down the floor. I'd score and you'd tell me I was lucky you had a cramp or I only scored because I stepped on your foot."

"You must have me confused with someone else," I said.

"I don't know where you're coming up with scoring thirty points, though. I don't think you stopped me the whole game. Matter of fact, you were whining to everybody on the floor; refs, players, I think you even complained to the lady running the concession stand."

I shrugged. "I think you're remembering it wrong, but if that's true, I must have not been getting any calls."

MaryAnn had her hip cocked. "Do you want me to just leave you here?" she asked.

"I'm sure they're showing a game at the bar across the street," I said, jerking my head toward the bar across the street. "You want to grab a beer while MaryAnn shops?"

I looked at MaryAnn. "Is that okay?"

"No, it's not okay," she snapped. "Josh, let's go."

"I guess not," he said, smiling.

"Give me a call if you put a team together," I said. "I'm sure MaryAnn has the number."

She glared at me without saying anything. "You called me less than two weeks ago to meet up for dinner," I said, feigning confusion.

"You're a lying asshole," she said, before stomping away.

"Okay, that was a lie," I said, once she was out of earshot. "But, seriously, give me a call if you put a team together."

I stuck out my hand and he shook it. "I will," he said.

I laughed as I walked back to my car, and kept laughing the whole way home. That evening, Amber and I were enjoying a nice candlelit dinner when the phone rang. Amber was closer so she answered.

"Hello," she said. A few seconds later, she handed the phone across the table, visibly upset. "It's your ex-."

I wiped my mouth with a napkin before taking it. "How did you get this number?" I asked.

"Don't mess with me by being friends with my boyfriend," MaryAnn said.

"How did you get this number?" I asked again.

"I'm serious. I know you're only trying to be friends with him to piss me off."

"I'm not messing with you by being friends with a guy who plays basketball," I said, more to Amber than MaryAnn. "If you don't want him playing basketball with me then tell him not to call. You're an expert at bossing boyfriends around."

"You don't want to piss me off. If he calls, tell him you can't play."

Amber was still staring at me, and I could tell she was trying to figure out if I was talking in code. I put MaryAnn on speaker. "So the only reason you called is because you don't want me to play basketball with your new boyfriend? If you swear to never call here again, I'll promise not to play basketball with him."

There was a pause. "Am I on speaker?" she asked.

"No, it's the phone," I said, shrugging at Amber.

"And I don't appreciate you saying that I was…"

I cut her off. "We have a deal or not?"

"Fine," she said after a few seconds. Without listening to anything else, I disconnected the line.

"She's like a bad penny," I said, handing the phone back to Amber.

She picked at her food for a few minutes, not saying anything. "You okay?" I asked.

She put her fork down and took a deep breath. "Promise you're not cheating on me."

I looked at the ceiling. "I swear to God I'm not sleeping with MaryAnn."

"Have you cheated on me like Dave said?"

"Why would I cheat on you? You give me everything I need."

She looked me in the eye. "And you've never cheated on me?"

I had to fight everything inside me not to look away. "I can't believe you're even asking me that," I said, maintaining eye contact.

She started to eat again, but I could tell she wasn't completely convinced. I tried to comfort myself with the fact that I hadn't lied, not really, anyway, but it didn't work. Amber deserved someone with character. The more I thought about it, the more I realized I didn't qualify. I stared at the ceiling for what seemed like hours that night before drifting off to sleep.

That conversation notwithstanding, things with Amber were going well. We got along, and we never fought. The fighting thing, though, was also a problem. Without it, there was no passion, no spark. I've always thought that a little arguing now and then was a good thing. Anytime Amber and I would even come close to arguing, her eyes would well up, and that would end it. And I hated the whole crying thing. To me, it was a form of manipulation. I would say something that she didn't like and the tears would start to fall.

With all the negatives, though, she was still good to me. She went out of her way each day, doing little things in an attempt to make me happy: a note here, a card there, buying a CD when I mentioned a song I liked. I knew beyond the shadow of a doubt that she loved me. It took my relationship with Amber to show me what I'd been missing. In fact, I barely thought of MaryAnn at all. The times I did, it was to feel sorry for the poor bastard she was turning into a pretzel.

For once in my life, I'd made the right decision. There was a time I had contemplated leaving Amber in an attempt to reunite with MaryAnn, but now I couldn't understand why I'd even considered it. I finally had stability.

The only problem was the pressure I got from practically everyone I knew to marry her. The more I thought about it, though, the more it made sense. One thing I knew for sure was that I would wait at least two years from the last time I was engaged. But even so, I knew I'd propose eventually. My last thought before drifting off to sleep was that I was happy.

Of course with my track record it couldn't last. The downfall started innocently enough. I was at work on a Thursday when Tonya told me that everyone in the office was going to karaoke and asked me to come along. I cleared it with Amber and she seemed pleased with the idea; said not to stay out late or drink too much, but to have a good time.

We all got there and sat at a table right in front of the dance floor. The only people in the office were women, and I'm sure I looked like quite the ladies man. We drank a lot of beer, and watched several people who couldn't sing make idiots of themselves.

Around ten o'clock, Tonya and I were the only ones left from our group. She asked me to dance, and we stayed out on the floor for four or five songs. At the beginning we were a fair distance apart, but the longer we stayed the closer we got. Toward the end, we were bumping and grinding.

After we sat down, she started rubbing my leg. Not long after I was doing the same. Her hand kept inching further and further up my thigh, and I started wondering what would happen next.

She leaned toward me. "I'm thinking of leaving my husband," she whispered in my ear. Talk about a scary moment. There was no doubt in my mind what was about to happen.

"Let's get out of here," she said. I thought that maybe we would have to call it a night since I lived with Amber, and she was still with her husband, but instead we sat in her car so long that the windows steamed up.

I kept trying to talk myself into leaving, but I couldn't think of a way to say goodbye. Next thing I knew, we were making out hot and heavy. Even then, I couldn't help focusing on her tooth. Other than my eyes, the rest of me did nothing to resist. A few minutes later, she had my pants down to my knees, and I could tell that she was about to get on top of me. I was drunk, but not that drunk. Sexually transmitted diseases scared the hell out of me. I pulled my pants over my hips.

"I can't do this," I said, buttoning them. "I have a girlfriend."

She looked at me for a few seconds, then pulled her shirt over her breasts and sat in the other seat. "Besides," I continued, "you're a married woman."

She stared at the windshield. "If you don't want to that's fine, but don't use that excuse."

I kept my mouth shut and opened the door. "I'll see you at work tomorrow," she said.

Tomorrow? Oh my God, what would I do tomorrow?

Sitting in Tonya's car had sobered me up a little, but not enough. I've always said that only idiots drive drunk, but that night I was one of those idiots. Luckily, I made it home safe.

In the parking lot, I checked my face in the rearview mirror to make sure none of Tonya's makeup had gotten on me. Amber was already in bed, and I lay beside her, careful not to wake her up.

The next morning at work, Tonya took me aside the moment I got in the door. "I'm sorry about last night," she said. "I've never done anything like that before."

"We were both drunk," I said, waving it off. "Things like that happen. Don't worry about it." That was the end of the conversation.

Unfortunately, it wasn't the end of the relationship. About two weeks later on a Wednesday night we were the only people left in the office. I was about to walk out the door when Tonya stopped me.

"You want to go for a drink?" she asked. Foolishly I agreed. We went to a bar down the street, and one thing led to another. We ended up back in the car where we started kissing and fooling around a little. It was still light outside, and since we obviously couldn't go to where either of us lived, we drove back to the plant. There were a couple janitorial people sweeping, but we went to the office and shut the blinds.

This time she was prepared. She handed me a condom, and we went at it right there on her desk. I couldn't blame the alcohol because I'd only had one drink.

It was a little after seven when I got dressed and hurried to my car. Tonya was leaning against it smoking a cigarette when I got there.

"You are a very bad boy," she said.

She leaned in to kiss me on the mouth, but I turned my head and she kissed my cheek. The moment was awkward to say the least.

"I have to get home, I said, avoiding eye contact and unlocking the door. She moved aside, and kissed me once more, and this time I let her kiss me on the lips.

Amber was in the kitchen making dinner when I got home. "I was starting to get worried about you," she said. "I thought I might need to send out a search party."

"Some of the people in the office talked me into having a drink," I said, walking into the bedroom to change.

I put on a pair of sweatpants and a t-shirt, and went back into the kitchen to help. Amber looked up and frowned. "You didn't drive drunk, did you?"

I held up two fingers on my right hand. "I only had one drink."

"Because all you need to do is call me and I'll be more than happy to pick you up."

I kissed her on the cheek. "I know, poodle."

Surprisingly I didn't feel all that guilty. There was no chance that what I had with Tonya would ever go beyond sex, and I didn't have to worry about her pressuring me for a relationship because she was already married.

The next day, Tonya acted like nothing had happened. She smiled a little more and would occasionally touch me in inappropriate places, but none of our coworkers had a clue. At least, I didn't think they did.

I'd like to say that was the last time we had sex, but it ended up happening quite a bit, most of the time during business hours. Tonya discovered a little walk-in closet that was completely hidden and out of the way. Usually we'd go down there during our lunch hour. It was a huge turn-on when we'd go back to our desks afterward and act like nothing had happened.

The odd thing is that we rarely talked, and that was kind of erotic, too. It made for fewer awkward moments. We'd go down to the closet separately, maybe a couple minutes apart. Then, with no foreplay at all we'd have sex for half an hour or so, and walk back.

I think it even improved my relationship with Amber. The empty feeling I had that related to passion was gone. Since I wasn't giving anything to someone else that would take away from our relationship, it was fairly uncomplicated.

Every time we would go to Amber's parents, her stepfather would go on and on about how much they liked me at the plant. He even mentioned the possibility of a raise within a few months. I was already making more money than I had at my last job, and it was nice to be somewhere I looked forward to going to work. Tonya had a lot to do with that as well. I never yearned for a woman like I did for her. It may have been the simplicity of the relationship, I don't know, but I looked forward to Monday, and I'd never done that with any other job.

Amber never suspected a thing because I was in no way detached. I looked at Tonya as being part of my work life, and I was always able to separate work from my home life.

Several months went by, and I began to think that Tonya and I were playing with fire. A couple times, coworkers would say they were looking for one of us during lunch. That led into the question of why we always seemed to take our lunches at the same time, but Tonya would always come up with an excuse. She was great at excuses.

I was a little worried that maybe she would break up with her husband and expect more from me, but she said that their relationship had dramatically improved.

It was coming up on November, and I was seriously considering proposing to Amber. I knew once I got engaged my escapades with Tonya would have to end. I was in the process of finding a ring when I got news that I never expected.

I'd been at work for maybe twenty minutes when Tonya came over to my desk.

"I need to talk to you," she said.

"Sure, what's up?" I asked, keeping it casual.

"In private."

She had talked a couple times about making amends with her husband so I figured it was that our liaisons were coming to an end. We walked down to our little closet, and the second she closed the door, she kissed me, first a little tentative and then with a lot more urgency. I started to cup her right breast, but she gently pushed me away.

"I know there hasn't been much more than sex between us, but I've grown to care about you over the last few months."

Uh oh. "Okay," I said, more as a question.

"So I don't want you to think that what we had doesn't mean anything."

"You're telling me it's over."

"Yes," she said, and then hesitated. "No," and then another pause. "I guess that's part of it."

I was thoroughly confused. "What exactly are you saying?"

She exhaled and there was another long pause. "What are you saying, Tonya?" I asked again.

"I'm pregnant."

The room became blurry, and I backed up until I was leaning against the wall, and then slowly slid to the floor. We'd been careful at the beginning, but after a while, condoms became too much of an inconvenience.

"I don't know if it's yours or my husband's."

We had been together every possible day during the last three months, but I saw a small glimmer of hope.

"So there's a chance it's his?" I asked, looking up.

"Not much of a chance, but it's possible. I've been with him a couple times over the last month or so."

"Are you having the baby?" I asked, head in hands.

She hesitated. "Yes."

There was another long pause. "But, no matter what happens, you're out of it," she said.

"How can I be out of it?" I asked, looking up. "There's, what, a ninety, ninety-five percent chance I'm the father?"

She shook her head. "It doesn't matter. I have two kids with my husband, and he's the father of this baby."

"So no matter what, I'm not involved?"

"Yes."

"I don't like the idea of my kid going around with someone else's last name."

She snorted. "You asking to marry me?"

"Yes, that's what I'm saying," I said, after taking a deep breath. "We should get married."

"And if the five percent comes through and my husband's the father, then what?"

She had me there. "Jesus, Tonya," I said.

"Like I said, this isn't something we're arguing about. I'm not leaving my husband, you're not leaving your girlfriend. This relationship never happened."

I finally nodded. "You're sure it's not open for debate?"

"I think it's great you're being so damn honorable about it, but yes, I'm sure."

I was really confused by the whole ordeal, and it took several weeks to come to terms with it. I figured that since I had absolutely no say in the matter, I'd have to accept her decision. Even though that gave me a measure of peace, it was still upsetting.

I thought I'd gotten through it when Amber called me at work and asked me to come home. It was a little before noon when she called, so I asked what was wrong. She said she wanted to tell me in person. My

The Amateur

heart was in my throat the whole ride home, and I ran through all of the possible scenarios. Had she found out that I had messed around? Was someone sick or dying? I rushed through the door, and Amber was standing in the living room.

"Sit down," she said, pointing at the couch with a tentative smile. "Do you want anything to drink; water or something?"

"What's wrong?" I know I must have sounded agitated and it only made her more nervous.

"I went to the doctor today."

"Are you sick? What's wrong?" I asked again, this time a little more scared.

"No, not that kind of doctor; I went to see my gynecologist."

At that moment, I knew what she was about to say. Talk about irony. Once good thing was that I'd already run the gamut of emotions that go along with that sort of thing.

"You're pregnant," I said.

She nodded, studying me closely. "So what do you think?"

This was definitely not a time for honesty. I cleared my throat. "I think it's great," I said with a smile. I stood up and started toward the kitchen. "I'll have that glass of water now."

"This doesn't mean we have to get married or anything like that," she said quickly.

I stopped walking and turned. "Seriously, I'm happy. I really am."

I walked back and wrapped my arms around her. "I love you," I said, staring at the ceiling.

"I didn't know how to tell you," she said, starting to cry, "I was worried you'd think I'd done it on purpose."

"I love you," I said again. "That never crossed my mind."

"I love you, too," she murmured.

I couldn't help but think she'd in all likelihood feel differently if she knew that another child might have the same father; a child who would probably go to the same school and maybe the same class as the one she carried.

Other than the obvious knowledge that I'd have to grow up and take on adult responsibilities, there was the matter of telling my parents. Of their five children, I was by far the biggest disappointment.

This would just confirm it. I called my mother and told her that Amber and I would be over in a few minutes. Both of my parents were sitting on the front porch when we arrived.

"Mom, Dad, we have some exciting news," I said, stuttering over the word 'exciting.' "You're going to be grandparents. Congratulations."

I could feel Amber shaking while they processed that piece of information. My mom gave Amber an affectionate smile and stood up to give her a hug. It almost made me start to cry. While Mom was hugging Amber, Dad looked me in the eye.

"You know what this means," he said in a low voice, almost a whisper. I nodded even though I had no clue. "You have to marry her."

"We haven't decided on that yet," Amber said, sounding tentative.

My dad looked at her, and then back at me. He had a stern look in his eye; the one that, even though I was thirty, still struck fear in my heart.

"That's between you two," he said, although his expression told me otherwise. Both of my parents made over Amber, Mom especially, and I could tell it made her feel better about the situation. It also made me proud that my parents were supportive. There was a good chance they'd have reacted differently if one of my sisters had gotten pregnant, but that didn't make me any less grateful.

Next, we went to tell Amber's parents. I was cautiously optimistic since they were fairly liberal, especially compared to mine. This time, Amber broke the news while I kept a plastered on smile in place. Her stepfather's reaction was far different than that of my parents.

"Is that the way I raised you?" he bellowed. He had been with Amber's mom since Amber was in the second grade. The childlike excitement she'd shown on the ride over was gone in a blink.

"No," she said, her eyes on the ground.

"Sir," I interrupted, "Amber is the nicest person I've met in my life. I think you and her mother did a hell of a job."

"Was I talking to you?" he asked, glaring at me. "Stay out of it."

He turned back to Amber. "How are you going to take care of a child?" he asked.

"I'll take care of it," she mumbled, eyes still on the floor.

"And you," he said, turning back to me, "how are you going to take care of my daughter?"

I looked him straight in the eye. "Mr. Northcutt, I love your daughter."

That one stopped him in his tracks and after a long moment, he shook his head. "I hope you two know what you're doing," he said.

And that was that. Once he walked away, her mother came up and gave us both a hug. "He's just worried about you," she whispered.

Chapter 17

We had dinner there, and although her stepfather was unusually quiet, he didn't say anything more about Amber's condition. Around eight o'clock we headed home, and were in bed less than an hour later. It had been an exhausting day. I turned off the light and was crawling under the covers when Amber touched my arm.

"Thanks for sticking up for me," she said. "I wouldn't have known what to say if you weren't there."

"That's one thing you'll never have to worry about again," I said, putting an arm over top of her. "I'll be with you forever."

And I meant it. I couldn't imagine a life without her.

Things were coming together for me. I had a job that I loved, a great girlfriend, and I was about to start a family. But I knew without a doubt that I didn't deserve it. I had betrayed Amber in the worst way a man could betray a woman. Not only with one woman, but three, and there was a good chance that one of those women was carrying my child. Even though I couldn't imagine cheating again, the fact that it was out there was more than enough.

Less than a month after Amber announced she was pregnant, I took another loan from my 401k account and picked out a ring. This time I didn't play any games. I took her to Nick and Tony's, her favorite restaurant, for dinner, and when we got home that night, I proposed by candlelight. That was the last I saw of her for over an hour. During that period, she called everyone she knew. It was gratifying to have a fiancé who was genuinely excited.

After I had gotten engaged with MaryAnn, she had kept it a secret, like she was embarrassed, and she hardly ever wore her ring. Once Amber got off the phone, we made love by the same candlelight that I had proposed.

About a month later, I ran into MaryAnn at the mall. She was with a guy, and we talked for less than a minute. I told her that I was engaged, and she said they were living together. It felt like I was talking to a stranger. Both she and I pretended to be upbeat about seeing each other, but there was no spark. Honestly, I didn't even find her all that attractive. As I was walking away, I thought about how I had jeopardized my relationship with Amber on numerous occasions to be with a girl who never truly loved me; who had treated me more like a security blanket than a boyfriend.

At that point, I had gotten over the whole issue of messing around. It was like someone else had done those things. I didn't even know that guy anymore. Looking at Amber, knowing that she loved me, seeing in her eyes that would never change made me truly happy. I was in love.

Like all good things, though, it had to end. Amber was about three months along and starting to show. I was completely content with my job, and the only thing that Tonya and I talked about was how her pregnancy was going.

It was a little after nine on a Thursday morning when Amber's stepfather asked me to take a walk. His tone implied it wouldn't be a pleasant meeting. I had been running late a few days earlier, and hadn't called to let anyone know why so I figured that was the reason he was upset.

His office was across the plant. I started to talk to him on the way, but there were machines going and assembly lines rolling so I figured it could wait.

Once we were in his office he shut the door and closed his blinds. After we had both sat down, he stared at me for what seemed like an eternity. I was getting ready to apologize for being late when he started talking.

"I've heard that you're messing around on my daughter," he said. Though the timing was horrible, I wondered why he always called Amber his daughter, and she referred to him as her stepfather.

"I'm sorry? What did you say?"

He nodded and continued to stare. "You cheated on Amber." Like he was telling me instead of asking.

"I don't know what you're talking about," I said, trying my best to sound offended. "The only person I can think of who'd even say that is her ex-boyfriend, Dave. He's the reason I got fired from my last job, and he's still obsessed…"

"It wasn't Dave," he said.

I racked my brain, trying to think of whom else there could be, but I drew a blank. "Then I have no idea who'd say it."

He leaned back in his chair and cocked his head. "You going to tell me the truth, son, or do you want me to paint you a picture."

I shrugged and maintained my incredulous expression. "Sorry is this is offensive, but I don't know what in the hell you're talking about."

"Tom Sullivan called me today."

"Wait a second," I interrupted. "I don't know any Tom Sullivan."

"Tom Sullivan is married to Tonya Sullivan."

I'm sure my eyes revealed total shock. "You see, Tom is the union leader at the Coke plant, and we've played golf together for the last ten years. Matter of fact, he's the reason Tonya was hired here."

I put my head in my hands, not looking up. The diatribe continued. "Apparently Tonya had an attack of conscience, and told Tom the truth, said she didn't know if the baby she's carrying is his or yours."

He let that soak in, and I finally raised my head, trying to look as apologetic as possible. "I didn't mean for it to happen. I really didn't. We got drunk, it was late…"

"She said it happened a lot."

Now was the time to lie. "I don't know why she'd say that because it only happened once. She told me she was pregnant and then begged me not to say anything. Just so you know, Mr. Northcutt, that was long before I proposed to your daughter."

He slammed his fist on the desk. "That's supposed to matter? My daughter is carrying your child and there's a chance another woman is doing the same. You want to tell me it happened before you got engaged and expect that to explain it away?"

"No, sir, of course not. But like I said, it only happened once, and I didn't expect it. If I had known what would happen I'd never have gone out with them in the first place." I was pleading now. "Amber is the best thing that ever happened to me."

He shook his head. "That's not good enough."

"I'll do anything. Anything. You name it."

"Tell Amber the truth."

I closed my eyes. "It would kill her."

"I don't want to have to look away from my daughter every time I see her for the rest of my life. Either you tell her or I will."

I stood up. "Please Mr. Northcutt. She and I have a life together. She's carrying my child. I swear on my soul it will never happen again."

He looked up at me for a long moment. "I can't take that chance. If she decides to stay with you after she knows the truth, that's her business."

"It would hurt her more if she finds out. Why do you want to put her through that?"

He seemed to mull that over, and I felt a spark of hope, but he shook his head again. "Maybe if you had told me the truth when I first asked you, maybe then I could believe you, but frankly I don't. Tonya says it happened on many different occasions, you say only one. But she's the one who spoke up and told the truth. In my book, that means her words carry more weight than yours."

"What if I quit?"

"That's up to you, son, but it doesn't change anything." He said, getting up and walking around his desk. "I'll give you until the end of the week."

I slammed his office door when I walked out, so hard that the concussion momentarily shut down some of the work in the factory. The thing I wanted to do most was throw something through a wall. The man claimed to care for his stepdaughter, yet he wanted to destroy her relationship with the father of her child; to utterly humiliate her.

Head down, I walked back to my department. I grabbed a medium-sized box from next to the copier and started filling it with things from my desk. Tonya made eye contact, but quickly looked away.

"Out of it, huh," I said.

"I'm sorry," she said quietly.

"Explain how me not saying anything turned into you making a confession."

"He said he knew I was cheating and wanted a paternity test once the baby was born," she said, staring at her desk.

I looked at her, head tilted back. "So he knows you're messing around, and you admit it. Sure, that makes sense. You want to get it out in the open, I understand that. The thing I'm trying to figure out is how my name came up."

"What do you want me to say?" she asked.

"You screwed up my life."

She rolled her eyes. "I didn't force you to sleep with me."

"Seriously, that's your reason?" I asked incredulously. "You didn't force me to sleep with you? At least say you two were talking about taking a trip to Texas, and that's so ironic because the guy who might be the father of your baby is named Houston."

"Don't give me that. You tried getting in my pants the day we met."

"Well, I sure didn't have to try very hard."

She started crying and after watching her for a few seconds, I walked over and gave her a hug. "I'm sorry," she said meekly.

"What happens next?"

She sniffled, and finally looked up. "He said as long as I was totally honest he'll stay with me and won't care if he's not the father."

"I guess you know my fiancé is pregnant."

She nodded. "Tom said he'll tell her if I don't," I said, rubbing the back of my neck. "I don't think she's going to be as understanding as your husband."

Tom chose that moment to walk in, and his eyes darted back and forth between me and Tonya.

"I think you better leave, son," he said.

"You see the box on my desk?" I asked, glaring at him. "I'm not packing all my stuff together for a trip to the bathroom."

"Get out of my factory," he bellowed.

"Funny," I said over my shoulder. "I don't remember seeing your name on the building."

The Amateur

I thought he might come after me, but I didn't hear footsteps. There was small chance that Amber's stepdad wouldn't tell Amber the truth, and after our conversation he'd probably tell her sooner rather than later. I tried to think of any possible way I could get out of saying anything. I could always say the woman was lying; that it was her stepfather who slept with her, and then blamed me. The more I thought about it, though, I realized that honesty was my only option.

On the way home, I bought a bouquet of roses and a box of Esther Price Chocolates. There was no easy of doing it, so I thought maybe buttering her up would help. I decided to be straightforward, and then let the chips fall where they may.

For the first time in a long time I was terrified. An act of stupidity could cause me to lose the best thing I'd ever had; sheer and utter stupidity, no other way to see it.

Amber was sitting on the couch, and her face lit up with a smile when she saw the flowers and the box of candy.

"You're so sweet," she said. She grabbed a vase from under the sink and added water, then put in the flowers.

"Thank you," she said, giving me a peck on the cheek.

I could feel my heart racing. "There's something I need to tell you."

She put the vase on the counter and then stepped back to admire it. "Okay," she said, still looking at the flowers.

"You probably need to sit down for this one."

She looked at me, and I guess she realized it was serious. She sat down and I got on my knees.

"You know I love you," I started.

Her face took on a quizzical expression. "Okay."

"And I would never do anything to hurt you."

"Why do I feel like you're about to hurt me?"

"Amber, I was stupid," I said, and I could see her eyes well up. "You're the only girl I've truly loved who I knew loved me back. I want to spend the rest of my life with you."

I sat there for a moment, knowing if I said anything more I'd start crying. "Say it," she said.

"I messed around," I said, my voice starting to break. "I didn't mean to, I swear I didn't, and it'll never happen again."

She started to cry, but neither of said anything. I tried to lean my head against her, but she pushed me away.

"I'll do anything," I said. "Anything. I swear to God. Please, Amber."

She said something in a low voice that I couldn't hear. "What?" I asked.

"I said get out of my house," she said, this time screaming it.

"Can't we talk about this?"

She pushed me away, and went to the door. "Get out," she said, opening it and pointing toward the street.

"I love you," I said, going over to where she was standing. I tried to give her a hug, but she pushed me away. The tears had stopped.

"If you loved me, you would have never cheated on me."

I looked at her again, and when our eyes met hers started to well up again. "I'm begging you," I said, "give me another chance."

She made a point of looking away. "Do you remember what you told me? Back at the beginning when you talked about your girlfriend cheating on you? You said that you knew it would never work between you and your ex- after you found out she cheated on you because you could never trust her again."

"This is different," I said, returning to my knees. "This wasn't something I planned. I went out with some people from work to have a few drinks, I got drunk, she came on to me, and it just happened."

"Cheating doesn't just happen."

"This time it did," I said, "and it will never happen again."

"I never cheated on you. Never. You know why? Because I don't put myself in a position where I have to say 'no.' First it's dinner, then it's a drink, then it's back to his place. If you say 'no' in the beginning, you don't have to worry about it."

"It was people from work," I said, gesturing wildly. "It was a new job. I was trying to get to know people better. I never dreamed anything like that would happen."

"Was she someone you work with?"

"I already quit."

"So it was someone you work with," she said, looking even madder. "Does my stepfather know?"

I nodded. "So he's the reason you're telling me now?" she asked.

I hesitated before nodding again. "You swore to me you'd never lie again," she said. "Do you remember that?"

I looked down. "Do you remember that?" she asked again.

"I remember."

"What did I say would happen if you lied to me again?"

"It's not like that. I didn't lie to you."

"You swore you'd never cheat on me, or did you forget that, too? You swore. Now get out of my house."

"The night of the holiday party you said that you'd never leave me even if I cheated. You made me promise not to leave no matter what, so I'll show how much I love you by staying and working this out."

"I was drunk," she screamed. "People say stupid things when they're drunk. You thinking that somehow justifies what you did makes it that much worse. I can't even stand the sight of your face right now. Leave, or I'll call the police."

I stood there for a long moment but it was obvious she wasn't going to change her mind. "I'm sorry," I said.

She held the door and for a few seconds and I thought she was going to ask me to come back in, but then she slammed it in my face. I stood there for a little while longer before going out to the parking lot.

I sat in the car for a minute or so, and then drove down the street to the closest bar. I got there around 6:30, and drank steadily until after midnight. I was falling down drunk when I called Amber from my cell.

"I'm down here at O'Malley's," I said when she picked up the phone.

"Are you drunk?"

I laughed a little. "Yeah, you could say that."

"Why are you calling me?"

The lines I'd rehearsed didn't seem nearly as good as they had a few minutes earlier. "I was hoping we could talk things out."

"I've already said all there is to say."

I tried a different tact. "You said if I was ever drunk to call you, and you would pick me up."

"That was before," she said after a brief period of silence. "You need to find someone else."

The next thing that happened was my cell phone went dark. I thought about calling her back, but instead called my brother, Rob, who after grumbling a little said he'd be there in a minute.

"You want me to take you home?" he asked when I got in the car.

"Yeah, your place," I said.

"You okay?"

"I don't want to talk about it," I said. The glass from the side window was freezing cold and felt good against my cheek.

"Amber kick you out?"

"I said I don't want to talk about it," I moaned.

"Did she catch you messing around?"

"God, Rob. I'm too drunk to talk about this right now. Ask me tomorrow."

He didn't say anything else. I don't remember how I got on the couch, but I woke up around two in the morning knowing I was about to throw up. I stumbled back to the bathroom and did my deed in the toilet until I was dry heaving. I lay on the floor, and the tile felt good against my face. I finally fell asleep like that, and woke up when my brother knocked on the door.

"What time is it?" I asked.

"It's a little after six. You okay?"

"Do I look okay? I'm still drunk, and right now I'd just as soon be dead."

"You want me to get you some water?"

I nodded and put my face back against the tile. He came back a few moments later with a big plastic cup.

"I have to work so you're going to need to get out of here," he said.

I took the water, and stumbled to the couch. I fell back to sleep, and my brother woke me up around seven. He stood there watching me, a smirk on his face.

"You going to tell me what happened?" he asked.

I rolled away from him. "She caught me with my pants down."

"With MaryAnn?"

I shook my head. "The chef girl?" he asked.

"No, a girl in the office. She told her husband who told Amber's stepfather, who made me tell Amber."

"Hold the phone. Husband?"

"I know it was stupid, okay?"

"I don't want to say I told you so…"

"Then don't," I interrupted. "I already know I messed up. I already know what a great girl Amber is and how everybody says over and over again how lucky I was."

"Did she ever find out about the other two?"

"I don't know what difference it makes now. What's she going to do, kick me out again?"

He took my cup of water and refilled it. "Was the married girl in the office hot?"

"She was all right, but the sex was incredible."

"Yeah?"

"You have to swear not to say anything." I said. "I mean really swear."

"Okay, I swear," he said, acting like I was making it too big of a deal.

"She's pregnant, too. She doesn't know if the father is me or her husband."

He started laughing like he'd never stop. Before long he was on the floor. He laughed so hard that after a while I couldn't help but laugh, too.

"It's really not that funny," I said.

"Are you kidding me? If it's not the funniest thing I've ever heard, it's easily top three."

"Don't you have to work?" I asked, lying back down. "I'm sure there's a line of people outside the pawnshop waiting to sell all the stuff they stole last night."

He looked me over. "I'll be back in four or five hours. You want me to pick something up?"

"Just let me sleep," I said, pulling the pillow over my head.

I vaguely remember the door closing, and then what seemed like five minutes later, someone was shaking me. I pulled the pillow down over my ears, but almost immediately it was yanked away.

"You need to go," Rob said, urgency in his voice.

My head was pounding and opening my eyes put me on the verge of throwing up. "Give me another hour," I groaned, burying my face in the couch cushion.

"Amanda is on her way over."

I slowly stood and felt an overwhelming wave of nausea so I sat back down. "Amber kicked me out, remember? I got nowhere to go."

"So go to the mission," he said, grabbing my shoes. "We'll be gone in half an hour so you can come back and shower then."

"God," I said, drawing it out. "At least let me hit the head."

"You can hold it," he said, but I walked back to the bathroom anyway. I was washing my hands when there was a knock on the front door.

Rob stuck his head through the crack in the bathroom doorway. "Mess this up again, and I'll kill you, swear to God" he whispered.

Amanda was sitting on the living room couch when I walked out. I acknowledged her with a brief smile and started putting on my shoes.

"Sorry, I'm not allowed talking to you," I said, looking down while I tied the laces.

"Why not?" she asked, more to Rob than me.

"Someone seems to think I'm a trouble-maker."

She laughed. "I can't imagine why he'd think that."

"So I have to go before, and I quote," I said, using the two fingers on each hand for emphasis, "'mess things up again.'"

"You don't have to leave," she said.

"Seriously?" I asked, looking at Rob.

He stared daggers at me. "Not unless there's somewhere you need to go," he said.

"I never got a chance to thank you," she said.

"Hear that, Rob?" I asked, jutting out my chin. "She wants to thank me."

"Don't break your arm patting yourself on the back," he mumbled.

"I would have never given him a chance if you hadn't come to the coffee shop that day," she said, smiling at Rob affectionately. "So thank you."

"You're welcome. And congratulations on the engagement," I said, and then gave a sideways glance at Rob, "or the vacation if you heard him wrong. I never thought that my brother would find such a beautiful girl."

"I'd be worried you were trying to hit her if she didn't already know you were a dog."

I looked around. "Speaking of dogs, where's Herbert?"

"He doesn't live here anymore," he said after a short pause.

I looked back and forth between them. "Then she knows?"

"He told me why he bought the dog, and I gave it to someone from work," Amanda said.

"I told her you wanted a dog your whole life," I said to Rob. "Thanks for throwing me under the bus."

"How was I supposed to know you told her that?" he asked defensively.

She laughed. "I never believed you anyway."

"Besides," he sniffed, "we tell each other the truth about everything."

"Everything, huh?" I asked. "Have you told her about the Latino guy you met in high school?"

Amanda laughed and turned to Rob. "A Latino guy?" she asked.

His face colored. "That's a lie."

"Nothing to be embarrassed about. A lot of guys do that when they're coming to terms with their sexuality. I never did, but…"

"This is exactly why I wanted you gone."

"Hey, where's the hostility coming from?" I asked. "I'm trying to say I admire how you had the courage to rebel against our societies puritanical standards.

"Besides, it only happened once." I paused. "At least that's what you told me."

"You are getting awful defensive," Amanda said, a playful smile on her face.

"Amanda," I said, giving her a reproachful frown. "What happens in Costa Rica stays in Costa Rica."

He glared at me, clearly not amused. "You want anything?" he asked Amanda once he opened the refrigerator.

"Hey, sensuous," I called out. Amanda looked at Rob and then back at me.

"Which of us were you talking to?" she asked.

"Are you kidding?" I asked incredulously. "Rob hasn't told you about 'hey, sensuous.' That's been his line since middle school. It's pretty clever, actually. It means 'sensuous up, get me another beer.'"

I leaned back. "Matter of fact, I think he came up with it on his own."

"She probably thought you were hitting on her," Rob said, handing her a Coke.

"No beer, sensuous?" I asked.

"Stop being an idiot. I don't have any beer in the fridge. You want a beer, the liquor store is right down the street."

"That's a joke, right? No beer?"

He just looked at me, not saying anything. "I guess you're more of a wine drinker now," I said, more as a question. He still didn't respond. "So do you got to art museums and eat the cubes of cheese with the toothpicks stuck in them?

"Are you ready?" he asked Amanda.

"Do you keep your smoking jacket in the closet next to your black turtlenecks?"

"You want to go through my closet now?"

"Uh oh," I said, raising my eyebrows. "Sounds like somebody's worried I'll find his Yanni records and his glasses with the black frames and rectangle-shaped lenses."

"It must be amateur hour," Rob said, looking sideways at Amanda. "Somebody give this moron a microphone."

"Maybe next time I come over to watch a game I'll bring a nice bottle of Chardonnay. We can have a wine-tasting at halftime."

Amanda looked back and forth between us. "Do you want me to step out of the room so you two can work this out?"

I held up a hand. "Before you go, I could really use a woman's advice," I said, moving to a love seat diagonal to the couch where she was sitting. "I have a situation with my girlfriend."

"This should be good," Rob said, settling in.

"Are you sure I'm qualified to give this kind of advice?" she asked.

"Well, you obviously believe in charity since you're engaged to Rob, and I need a woman who thinks charitably."

"He might be a big dork, but he's definitely not a charity case," she said, squeezing his knee.

"The thing is, she caught me in a delicate position," I said, choosing my words carefully. "I tried to apologize, but she kicked me out."

"How delicate?"

"She found out I was messing around. I mean, I'm not messing around now," I quickly clarified. "This happened, like, four or five months ago. I was thinking, with her being pregnant and all, maybe she'd come around after she settles down a little."

"Tell her the best part," Rob chimed in.

I glared at him. "I seem to recall the part of our conversation where you swore not to say anything."

"The other girl's pregnant, too," he said, and started laughing.

"Yeah, that's the part you swore you wouldn't repeat."

"My dumbass brother knocked up two women at the same time."

"It's not for sure the baby's mine," I said defensively.

"And she's married, too," he said. "Tell her about that."

"You can't keep your mouth shut about anything."

"She needs to know the whole story to give any advice," he said wisely.

"And she knows all this?" Amanda asked.

I hesitated and then slowly nodded. "Not good," she said.

"If it was you, you wouldn't take me back, not even if it happened almost six months ago?"

"I don't know a girl in the world who would."

"Not even if I buy her two dozen roses and get on my knees and beg?"

She shook her head. "Not even if you dug a hole to China."

Rob laughed. "I was just wondering how you would work out visitation. Would you have both kids on the same weekend or would you switch? Or maybe you could pick the one up after you dropped the other off."

"What about the dog?" I asked. "How are you working out visitation with Herbert?"

"Hey, look on the bright side. Parent-teacher conferences will be pretty easy. You'll be able to take care of both at the same time."

"You're an idiot," I said.

"And I know you quit your job. You think you'll get conjugal visits if they throw you in jail for not paying child support?"

Amanda gave him a reproachful frown. "That was out of line."

I looked away and then back at him. "Anybody else says that, I beat their ass."

He snorted. "You've never won a fight in your life."

"Not true," I said, standing up. "Absolutely not true. Nate Fuson, third grade."

"He beat your ass."

"See, you say that, but that's not what happened. The only good shot he had was when you grabbed my arms."

"He had you on the ground," he said, saying it like I was crazy. "He'd have probably killed you if I hadn't made him stop."

I paused. "I forgot about that, but that's not the point. I can't believe you said that about me and Amber."

"Or you and the girl with the tooth."

I glared at him. "You're an asshole."

"And I'm the only thing between you having a place to stay and being homeless."

"So, seriously, you think I have a chance to get her back?" I asked.

He laughed. "What I think is that I have a roommate for a while."

I looked at Amanda, and she nodded. A few minutes later they left, and I was alone. Part of me believed that Amber would take me back eventually, but I wasn't sure. In all honesty, I wasn't sure of anything. I tried to call her, but got the machine so I hung up without leaving a message. About an hour later I called again, this time leaving a message letting her know where I was staying.

Around six o'clock that evening there was a knock on the door. I opened it since my brother was still gone, and found all my stuff boxed up on the welcome mat. I ran into the parking lot and saw the taillights of Amber's Civic. I started to run after her, but she was gone by the time I had taken a few steps.

After two weeks of leaving unreturned messages, I drove to her place. She looked tired when she opened the door.

"I tried to call," I said.

She started to close the door, but I stopped it with my hand. "The reason I never called you back is because I don't want to talk to you," she said.

"Do you still love me?"

She stopped pushing, and stood off to the side. I walked in and waited, but she didn't respond.

"Do you love me?" I asked again.

"Yes."

"Do you miss me?" I asked, touching her face.

She let my hand linger there for a few seconds before pushing it away. "I could never forgive you," she said.

"I wouldn't forgive me either."

She walked over to the couch and sat down. "I don't know what to do, Houston," she said, starting to cry.

I sat beside her. "Give me a chance and I'll spend the rest of my life making it up to you."

I vaguely remembered hearing that somewhere and hoped it wasn't something I'd said before. She rested her head on my shoulder.

"It'll never work," she said. "There's no way I could ever trust you again."

"I'm the father of your child," I said.

"From what I hear, this isn't the only child you have. Are you going to tell her the same thing?"

I closed my eyes. "I love you. More than I've loved anyone my whole life. Even more than I love myself. I don't work without you."

She sat up and pushed me away. "You can still be a part of the baby's life is you want. I'll leave that up to you."

"Didn't you hear what I said?" Pleading now. "I love you."

"I heard you, Houston, but it doesn't matter. Nothing you can say will change my mind."

She was right. There was nothing I could say.

Epilogue

It's been several months since that conversation took place, and there's still nothing I can say. I haven't heard from Amber, but from what I understand she's due to have the baby at any time.

I've thought a lot about all that happened both with MaryAnn and Amber, and I have many regrets. I've tried to get a hold of Amber's family, but they won't accept my calls. I have a lot of reasons to apologize. They welcomed me into their home and treated me like family. Hell, her stepfather even got me a job when I needed one. They gave me everything a man could ask for, and I betrayed their trust in the worst conceivable way. I would like to find a way to at least have her forgive me, but I've given up any hope for reconciliation. She was right. There's nothing I can do to make her forget.

I thought I could have it all, but I ended up with nothing. Looking back, I got what I deserved. Some people are destined to be alone; people like me. I've come to realize that in the game of love, I'm just an amateur.

Coming Soon

A Life in Review

by Robert Ledford

Excerpt Follows

Grandpa

It started like any other late summer day in the Ohio Valley. The temperature was in the high seventies and the humidity was stifling when I got out of bed at six a.m. I had gone to sleep with the fan blowing full blast, but with no air conditioning in the house I don't think I managed more than a couple hours of sleep. It was the middle of August, less than two weeks before the start of my senior year in high school.

My grandfather and I had a tradition of going out to Kincaid Lake every Tuesday during the summer. Grandpa is big on tradition. He'd pick me up around six-thirty and we'd drive the hour or so to the lake, and then fish until around noon. I'd never been much of a morning person, and when the alarm went off I thought it was a tradition I'd just as soon end. I never much enjoyed fishing, especially under a hot sun. It wasn't so bad in late spring and early summer, but during the dog days of August I dreaded it.

If it had been anyone else, I'd have begged out of going, but I couldn't say "no" to my grandfather. He'd been my hero since before I could walk. Even though he was closing in on seventy I still saw him as being larger than life. His hair had a little silver now, but there was more black than gray. He was a big, powerful man in his youth and even though he'd slowed down a little, he was still everything I wanted to be: strong, respected, and charming. It didn't hurt that I was his favorite. Once in a while, my father would complain that Grandpa chose to spend more time with me than him. There was always a twinkle in his eye when he said it, but I could tell there was some resentment in there as well.

After getting out of bed I ate a quick breakfast and dressed in a pair of shorts, a thin long-sleeved shirt, and a raggedy pair of tennis shoes. The long-sleeves were so my arms and shoulders wouldn't burn. I didn't get a shower, knowing that I'd need one when I got back from the lake.

At exactly six-thirty, my grandfather would pull into the driveway and honk his horn. He never came to the door; he'd just honk and stay in the car no matter how long it took for me to get out there. My parents and siblings were still sleeping so I closed the door behind me as quietly as I could.

"You're looking good, Zeke," Grandpa said, a little smirk on his face. My grandfather is the only person who has ever called me by that name. My given name is Ezekiel Paul Kolacka. I was named after an Old Testament prophet in the Bible. My father is a Baptist preacher, and he's very big on Biblical names. I have four siblings, and we're all named after obscure Bible characters.

I don't look much like a Zeke. I'm tall and skinny, even though I've filled out over the last few years.

My grandfather was decked out in his usual fishing garb: grey tank top, baggy tan shorts topped off with an army green fishing hat that looked about a hundred years old. His car was an old brown two-tone Lincoln Continental that he'd owned as far back as I can remember.

"You, too, Pops," I said, grinning.

The lake was about an hour away, and the drive was my favorite part of our time together. My grandfather would tell me all kinds of stories from his past, and even though he told the same ones over and over, I never got tired of hearing them. He had fought in Korea, and he loved to talk about the war; how crazy everyone was, the time he almost got shot by one of his buddies, the K-Rations that everyone complained about, but he thought were the tastiest thing he'd ever eaten; sometimes we'd sit in the car after we got to the lake when he got on a roll.

"You still going to that private school?" he asked, a little contempt in his voice when he said the word "private." He knew full well where I went, but he loved to talk about my private education and how it limited my opportunities. That was another thing that drove my father crazy. My father and grandfather didn't have a whole lot in common when it came to things like that. It was amazing how similar they were in some areas, but polar opposites in others.

"Bunch of stuck-up trust fund babies," he muttered. Obviously I had told him some stories as well.

"It's not so bad anymore."

"Yeah?" he asked, glancing over. "You got your eye on any of those cake-eaters?"

I shrugged. "Not yet. We'll see."

He was always asking me about girls, and if I'd had my way with any of them. I think it was his way of trying to live vicariously through me.

"You decided where you're going to college?" he asked.

"Bowling Green has sent me stuff about a scholarship, so if that comes through I'll probably go there."

"Your dad trying to talk you into going to a Bible college?"

I rolled my eyes. "Nonstop. He keeps reminding me that I can go to some of them for free since he's a preacher."

He laughed. "From what I understand, colleges are full of young pretty girls."

"You can always come visit," I said, sneaking him a sly grin. "I can introduce you around if you want, tell all those girls you're my uncle."

He slapped my leg. "You say that like it's a joke, but you might change your mind when I show up with my suitcase."

The talk went on like that for another half hour or so, and then he launched into another string of stories. I sat in the car with the window down wondering why I had been dreading the trip.

We parked as close as we could to the dock and walked the hundred feet or so to where his boat was tied. The boat was a blue and white twenty-eight footer with an old Johnson motor.

Once we got out on the lake and threw our lines in the water, conversation ended. I got a Coke out of the cooler and leaned back, just enjoying the sound of the water lapping against the boat. By nine o'clock Grandpa had caught three nice-sized bass, and I'd only caught one blue gill that I had to throw back. I noticed he kept grimacing and rubbing his left arm, but I didn't think much of it. He was reeling in another fish when he gave a loud gasp and slumped over. I dropped my pole and scooted toward him.

"You okay, Pops?" I asked.

"Get us back to the dock, Zeke," he whispered. Now I was panicking. I drove the boat back as fast as I could and tried to get as close to the edge as possible. Even though it was someone else's spot I pulled in and rammed the boat hard into the wall. A guy a little further down the dock almost fell into the water. I looked over at my grandpa, and his eyes were closed. It didn't look to me like he was breathing.

"What's wrong with you, boy?" the man who I'd almost knocked into the water asked.

"There's something wrong with my grandpa," I said, trying to pull Grandpa out of the boat. "I need to get him to a hospital."

The angry look on his face disappeared the moment he saw my grandfather. He whipped a cell phone out of a case on his belt and punched in a few numbers.

"I think I have a guy who's either had a heart attack or a stroke," he said. There were a few uh-huh's and all right's, and he gave our location before turning it off.

"They'll have someone here soon," he said.

I kept trying to wake Grandpa up, but he wouldn't respond. I grabbed him around the shoulders and tried to lift him and carry him to the car, but he wouldn't budge. I was really panicking now. The man who called 911 was saying something, but I wasn't listening. I just sat there holding my grandfather, hoping against hope that it was a crazy dream, and that in a minute I'd wake up and everything would be okay. I started crying, rocking him back and forth trying to get him to respond.

An ambulance pulled up about ten minutes later and two men carted him in a stretcher up the steps of the dock and into the back of the ambulance. I begged one of the EMT's to let me ride along, but he refused.

I ran to Grandpa's Continental, but realized I didn't have the keys when I got behind the wheel. I sat down, my back against the car and cried. I don't know how long I sat there, but the man who called the ambulance walked over.

"You okay, son?"

I shook my head, my hands still covering my face. "I can't get to the hospital."

"Do you know where they're taking him?" he asked, and I shook my head. "The only hospital in the area is St. Anthony's. I'll drive you if you want."

I wiped the tears from the face with the back of a hand. "Thanks," I said, feeling stupid.

We walked over to where his pick-up truck was parked. We didn't say a word to each other during the entire drive. He pulled up to the emergency room entrance and I opened the door.

"Sorry about almost knocking you into the water," I said, closing the door behind me. I could tell he was saying something, but I was too busy running toward the revolving door. There were a couple people standing in line at the registration desk, and the nurse was going over someone's forms, but I moved in between them.

"I think my grandpa had a heart attack," I said. "Can you tell me where he is?"

The nurse looked at me for a long moment, obviously irritated. Someone behind me said something about being rude and I turned around.

"My grandpa had a heart attack right in front of me, asshole," I said, wanting to punch him in the teeth.

I started to choke up as I turned back to the nurse. "Can you please just tell me where he is? Please?"

"What's his name?" she asked softly.

"Ernie Kolacka."

She punched his name into the computer and then stared at it for a few seconds. "If you'll take a seat, one of the doctors will be out shortly," she said.

I stood there, knowing what that meant, but not being able to accept it. I wanted to demand seeing him, but instead I sat down. I waited for several minutes and then I remembered my parents. There was a pay phone a few feet away and I got a couple coins out of my pocket as I walked over.

"I think Grandpa had a heart attack," I said when my mother answered.

"Where are you?"

I looked around. "I'm at St. Anthony's Hospital. I think he had a heart attack."

"We'll be there as soon as we can," my mom said.

"One minute he was fine, the next he slumped over. I think he might be…" I couldn't say it.

"We'll be there soon." I could tell she wanted to be comforting, but I couldn't take it. I didn't want her to hang up.

"What should I do, Mom? I don't know what to do."

"Just sit tight, okay? You don't know what it is. He might be okay. Just sit tight and we'll be there soon."

The doctor came out about five minutes later and he called out my grandfather's name.

"Where is he?" I asked. "Is he okay?"

He stared at me for a long moment and then looked past me. "Are your parents here?"

"I'm the only one. Is he okay? Can I see him?"

He stared at me a little longer, not saying anything. "Do you know when your parents will be here?" he asked finally.

At that moment I knew, not a doubt in my mind. I closed my eyes and stumbled over to a chair. I had thought my grandfather was indestructible. There was no way he could be gone. A few hours earlier he'd been fine, telling me how much better he was as a fisherman.

I had a lump in my throat so big I could barely breathe. The doctor followed me to where I was seated.

"He's dead, isn't he?" I asked, looking up.

He didn't say anything. "Can't you tell me that much? For God's sake, I was there. I saw him. I was there, okay? I'm not an idiot. I'm not a child. Tell me," I said, pleading now.

He nodded his head slowly. "We did everything we could."

I put my hands over both eyes and nodded. "Can I see him?"

"I'm afraid that's not possible," he said in a quiet voice.

I wanted to punch a wall, someone, anything. It was such a powerless feeling. The doctor sat down and put his hand on my shoulder. "I'll stay with you until your parents arrive."

I started crying when he touched me. I wanted him to hold me, squeeze me tight. I wanted to tell Grandpa I loved him, that he was the most important person in my life. I wanted to tell him he was my hero and that I'd always remember him.

I could see the doctor checking his watch every few minutes. I thought about telling him that he could go, but I didn't want to be alone.

My parents got there about forty-five minutes later, and my father's face was drained of color when he came through the door. The doctor stood to greet him.

"Is my father okay?"

"He's dead," I said before the doctor could answer. Tears sprang to Dad's eyes and he sat down in a chair.

"Your father had a massive coronary," the doctor said. "We did everything we could, but it was too late. I'm sorry."

My mother put her hand on Dad's shoulder and then wrapped her arms around his neck. I went over to join them. As the doctor walked away my mother looked up. "Are you okay?" she asked.

I shook my head. "I saw it, Mom. I watched him die. I wanted to do something, but I didn't know what to do."

"It's not your fault," my dad whispered.

"I'm sorry," I said.

"Your grandfather loved you more than anything," Dad said. "If he could pick anyone to spend his last moments with, it would have been you."

My father broke down then, and as he leaned against my mother's shoulder his cries turned to sobs. In that moment, I realized that I hadn't really known him at all. I had always seen him as a stern disciplinarian, a provider, a protector. Seeing him collapsed in my mother's arms, I realized he was more than just a father, he was also a man.

The funeral was a few days later, and the church was so full of people that some of them had to stand outside. My grandfather would have said it was a big waste of time.

I still think about that summer and how it changed my life. It was the summer I came to realize my mortality. It also changed my relationship with my father. I vowed to never take him for granted again, and Grandpa's death brought us a lot closer. I think Grandpa would have liked that.

CPSIA information can be obtained
at www.ICGtesting.com
Printed in the USA
FSOW01n0638251116
27797FS